The House

The House

M L Jones

Copyright © 2016 M L Jones
All rights reserved.

ISBN-13: 9781522991489
ISBN-10: 1522991484

To Angela and Gary Leighton-Jones: you have always been there to help me pick up the pieces through life and guide me through steps I have taken, even if I have gone against your advice. Hope this makes you proud.

Your loving son,

Mark Leighton-Jones

1

Llyn Alwen, a small natural lake about five kilometers long, sat upon Denbigh Moors in North Wales. Large conifer forests surrounded its shores. On a sunny day, the lake would sparkle like an oddly shaped emerald, casting out its ocean-blue rays into the world, the surface of the water undisturbed. Today, however, it was not a sunny day. It was gloomy, the rain freckling down from above. For the Moore family, it was not the best weather to start off their lives at their new family home.

The Moores were a normal-size family. Raine Moore was the eldest child, being eight. She had long, wavy blond hair, with an adorable, cheeky smile that could make her father's knees weaken every time he saw it. She had chocolate-brown eyes inherited from her father. Ivy Moore was the baby of the family. She was four. She had shoulder-length brown hair that lay straight. Her best features, however, were her blue eyes, like a perfect summer sky; you could often catch her mother staring into them.

Douglas Moore, in his own words, was the head of the household, an assertion that was heavily disputed. Doug and his wife, Joanne, would squabble most weeks about this.

Doug would stand in the kitchen, pushing out his chest importantly. "I'm the boss of this house. I wear the trousers," he would say, pride oozing from him.

"I let you think you're the boss, but really I'm the one driving," she would joke, which in turn would start off a twenty-minute debate.

Doug was a simple man. If he were asked to describe himself, he would say he was an easygoing, happy-go-lucky type of guy. Doug was only thirty-three with a stocky but not athletic figure. He kept his appearance simple too; he would only wear casual clothes and kept his dark-brown hair short to the sides with a bit of length on top.

Joanne Moore, on the other hand, was a different kettle of fish. She had to look good. She would obsess in the mornings, spending most of her time applying makeup to cover her naturally pale complexion. She had strawberry-blond hair that flowed down, clinging to the curves in her slim physique. Joanne hated her hair. It would never stay straight and was always, in her words, "curly and messy."

The Moores seemed to be your average family on the surface, with Joanne working as a receptionist for a local dental surgery office in the small town of Denbigh, a short fifteen miles away from their new home. However, appearances can be deceiving. Doug had recently been let go from his job at the bank, where he worked as the manager. The strain that losing his job had put on the family was immense. It caused frequent arguments, which left the children crying themselves to sleep most nights.

The House

But that wasn't the whole of it. The issues facing him had turned Doug to alcohol. The alcohol had consumed him. Most days he would be drunk, lying around their previous two-bedroom terrace house within a run-down housing estate. However, "the incident," as Doug and Joanne called it, had changed their lives for good, forcing them to look for a home elsewhere. They put their house up for sale and could not believe their luck when they found their new home situated by the shores of Llyn Alwen.

The Moores drove along the wet roads, rain now lashing from the heavens onto the tarmac and earth below. Doug sighed. "What a lovely day," he said, forcing a fake smile toward Joanne.

She laughed at him, her face ablaze with excitement. "Darling, it could be so much worse."

He nodded in agreement. They came along to the sign that was placed in the water-sodden grass verge. Doug turned right off the main road onto a dirt and gravel track, which led its way into one of the many woodlands that surrounded Llyn Alwen.

The track was unbelievably bumpy; the children bounced in their car seats. At one point the tip of Doug's head smacked the top of the roof lining. The track was not well situated for Doug's Volvo S40, with every bump causing the car's suspension to bang and groan as its wheels slammed into the earth. Doug continued down the track, and soon their new home came into view.

The house was a two-story country house built upon an old stone foundation that had recently been renovated to a gleaming white-coated finish. The roof was made of gray Welsh slate taken from the Blaenau Ffestiniog slate mines. Leading down to the house, through a wooden swinging gate, was a long dirt driveway that opened into an ample gravel courtyard. The lawn contained a large patch of grass with a large wooden picnic table and a child's swing set off to one side.

Doug pulled into the driveway and came to a stop outside the house. Towering over the house was an ancient, thirty-foot-tall oak tree with different platforms of branches sticking out at odd angles. Doug was first to exit the car, taking a large intake of air. "Ahhhh, nothing better than the country air," he said, drawing in another breath. He walked to the other side of the car and opened Joanne's door. The couple hugged as they looked up at their new home. Leading up to the porch was a stairway rotted by woodworms. The porch was long, with piles of leaves scattered across the floorboards. To the side of the front door was an old, weathered rocking chair.

The large front door was oak paneled, with two square windows carved into the top sections of the door. Along the porch were five ground-floor bay windows. The front was dull, with poorly chosen colors. *A bit of decoration and some nice coloring will change all that,* Doug thought to himself while inspecting the paint. He ran his hand along the walls, paint peeling away from the wood. His family stood on the porch, awaiting Doug to lead them through the front door. "Kids, welcome to your new home. We're going to be very happy here," he said, beaming from ear to ear.

The House

Doug placed his hand on the door and pushed against it. The door creaked as it opened slowly, revealing the front hallway. The hallway was long and wide. The walls were a dull pastel-green color. Along one wall was a long smear of dirt. Doug turned to his wife. "I don't remember that being there. Do you?"

She looked at the large stain on the wall and shook her head. "I would have definitely noticed that when we came to look at the place." She rubbed her hands over the smear mark. She looked at her hand and saw that the dirt was fresh. She shrugged and turned to Doug. "Darling, we only paid a hundred thousand pounds for this house. I don't think having to do some home improvements is such a bad thing."

Doug turned back to the remainder of the hallway, which had old-fashioned pictures hanging on the walls. One picture really caught his eye. The picture was large and hand painted; the lake was in the background.

In the foreground, a family stood near the lake, posing for the picture. Doug first noticed the man, tall and handsome, wearing a long fabric overcoat with what Doug thought was a farmer's cap. Next to him stood his wife, Doug assumed, wearing a long, old-fashioned lace dress and a sun hat. Her smile appeared genuine, with just a hint of naughtiness. With them were two children. A boy stood in shorts and a blazer, and a little girl, who must have been about the same age as Ivy, wore a dress similar to her mother's and had a delightful headband in her wavy brown hair.

Doug smiled at the picture. They appeared to be a nice, normal family from the picture. Doug moved on into what he had called the study-slash-reception room since he had first seen it a short three weeks ago. The room was generous in size. The walls were buried behind six large bookcases packed tight from corner to corner, with dusty old books that looked like they had been there for twenty to thirty years, untouched. The old owners or the ones before them had left a complete seating area. Three large brown leather settees were arranged around a small dark-mahogany coffee table. Dotted around the room, bringing extra light to it, were several candle-shaped lamps.

Doug walked around the room and grinned to himself. "This room is perfect for me. I can get a little desk and have my computer in here."

Joanne walked over to the marble mantelpiece situated on the far wall. "We will need a lot of wood to keep this house warm in the winter," she said, running her finger over the dusty marble. "Think I'll need my duster."

Doug pulled up his sleeves and looked at his watch. It was twenty past four in the afternoon. "Joanne, you get the kids settled. I'll get all the bags from the car," he said, clapping his hands in excitement. For the next two hours, Doug walked back and forth from the car into the house, depositing boxes of clothes, his computer, and Joanne's massive box full of cosmetics and hair products on the floor in the hallway and study. Joanne took the kids upstairs and introduced them to their new room.

The House

Doug could hear them playing and laughing while running around in the room and the sound of feet banging on the floor, knocking the dust off as they went.

Doug took a seat in the large dark-blue armchair, lay back in the seat, and began to scan the room. The air was cold where he sat. A sense of despair overcame him for a brief period. The inner demons began to stir, his inner voice slowly coming to the surface of his conscious mind. The hairs on his neck and arms began to rise, and his hands began to shake. He looked down at his hand, which was trembling uncontrollably. The world around him began to spin wildly, causing his head to pound like a second heart.

Doug stood up from the chair and threw his arm out toward the closest bookcase, steadying his balancing. "You need to fight this, Doug no more of this nonsense," his inner conscience said to him.

The inner voice chuckled in his head. "You will never be able to fight me. Nothing you do will ever rid you of me." Doug fell to the ground, holding both hands on his head in agony. The rushed footsteps of Joanne could be heard flying down the stairs. She found the twitching body of her husband.

"Oh my god, Doug. Are you all right?"

The inner voices stopped. He regained his senses slightly, with his hands still shuddering and his head beating away.

Joanne knelt down and placed her warm hand on Doug's forehead. It was ice-cold to the touch. "Oh, Doug. Come on. I'll help you up."

Without being able to control himself, Doug felt the rage ripping through his veins and coursing toward his fists, causing them to clench. He threw himself away from her like a bull that had been caged against its will. "Get away!" he shouted, storming away into the hallway, leaving Joanne kneeling on the floor, her face white with shock.

Doug threw himself out the front door and walked toward the car. He ripped the keys out of his pocket and jammed the key into the trunk lock. The trunk made a clunking sound. He lifted the trunk to block the view of any eyes watching him from the house. Doug peered into the trunk and lifted the spare tire, revealing a small bottle of Smirnoff vodka.

He felt his heart skip a beat at the sight of the alcohol. The thirst for it was overpowering, taking over his senses. The sound of the world disappeared, and his sole vision was on the bottle in front of him. His body temperature rose, and his skin began to sweat in expectation of consuming the vodka. He grabbed hold of the bottle. He unscrewed the cap. His mouth became dry, as if he had been in the desert for a day and this was water that would quench his thirst.

He raised the bottle to his lips. A tear of guilt rolled down his cheek. He took four gulps of the vodka. Its essence ran through him and took control of all his nervousness. His hands stopped shaking. His head cleared as if a mist had lifted from it. His vision went back to normal, and he once again heard the sounds of the local birds. The sweat evaporated into the air, as if it had not been there in the first place. Any anger he had felt disintegrated. He felt happiness again. The

The House

depression lifted and floated away into the air around him. Doug felt great. It then hit him, however. *I've just drunk,* he said to himself. He placed the bottle back under the spare and slammed the trunk shut.

He looked up at the house and saw Joanne standing on the porch with a look of sheer concern, her face white as a sheet and her eyes like pins as she watched him from a distance. Doug ran over to her, knowing what he had done was totally unforgivable. As he drew closer to her, he could see that she had tears in her eyes. He wasn't sure if they were they tears of sadness or fear. "Sweetheart, I'm so sorry. I don't know what came over me. My head went all funny," he said as he threw his arms around her, placing her in a bear hug.

He stood there holding his wife for at least five minutes as she buried her head in his chest, crying. "Please don't do that again. I have never seen you like that before," she sputtered while wiping tears from her cheeks. Doug felt an enormous amount of guilt for speaking to Joanne like he had earlier and for taking a drink. He had gotten away from his old life to stay away from alcohol, but his old demons were still not shying away. He had to get this under control, not for his sake, he knew, but for the sake of his family and its future.

Later that night, the early events of the day had been forgotten. The family had unpacked most of their possessions, with the exception of a few boxes that still needed to be unpacked and distributed around the house. That night Doug prepared his family's favorite: spaghetti Bolognese. He made this using tender, lean minced beef, which he placed in a scalding-hot pan and cooked with garlic and parsley. He added a fruity wine to the meat, which slowly evaporated, permeating the kitchen with its warm, welcoming aroma.

The dining room was situated on the far end of the house, with a staircase at the far end of the room that had planked stone steps leading down into the main living room. The dark-stained oak dining table was formidable in size, surrounded by eight high-standing oak chairs with mustard-colored fabric inserts. The walls were, for the moment, a dark, depressing gray. Joanne reassured Doug that they would not be this color for very long. Like the hallway, the dining room was home to numerous paintings. One of them again caught Doug's eye, as it depicted the same family as the one he had noticed in the hall. In this picture, the family was standing in the garden. The parents each had one arm around the other's shoulders and the other around one of the children at either side. The dining room was well lit by several candle lamps attached to the walls, casting large amounts of light across the room, leaving no hiding place, not even for shadows to hide.

Doug brought in the feast he had prepared for his family and placed the plates of food down on the table, seating himself at the head of the table. Joanne sat directly opposite him at the other end. The two children sat on either side of them. The family dug in to the meal. The children, as usual, got sauce all over their faces. Joanne would moan every couple of minutes because of this. "I just cleaned that dress, Raine," she hissed toward her daughter, after Raine dropped a large dollop of sauce on her dress.

The House

"So," Doug said, trying to steer the conversation elsewhere, "what do you think of your new room, Princess?" He looked at Raine. Raine was his firstborn, and he had always called her Princess since she was an infant.

"I love it, Daddy! I want a new bed, though. I don't like the one that I have to sleep on. I want a princess bed," she said, using her mother's eyelash-fluttering technique.

Doug had always felt outnumbered by his family, as he was the only man. He always lost when it came to something that one of the girls wanted, whether it was Joanne or one of the children. He took another mouthful of his supper and sighed. "Once we have settled in, Princess, we can get you and your sister a new bed, OK?" he said, nodding his head up and down really fast.

Raine smiled with excitement.

"What about you, Ivy? Does Daddy's little girl like her new bedroom?"

Ivy looked up at her father with her blue eyes. They gave the sense that she wasn't completely ok.

She shook her head, a tear rolling down her left cheek. "I want to sleep with you tonight, Daddy," she said, looking down at her food.

Doug saw this and moved to sit next to his child on the side of the table. He put his arm around her and brought her in for a reassuring cuddle. "What's the matter, Ivy? What are you scared of?"

She looked up at him again with tears in her eyes. "It's Tabitha, the little girl who lives in my room. She's in my bed. She told me she doesn't like me."

Doug looked at Joanne, concerned. "There was a girl in your bed? When was this?"

"Before, Daddy. She was lying in my bed. She screamed at me, telling me to leave."

Doug looked into his child's eyes. He knew that children had wild imaginations, but she appeared to be serious about what she had seen. He knew there wasn't a girl in her bed she was just imagining things from the stress of moving to a new home and leaving behind what she was used to. It was hard for children to adjust, especially children Ivy's age. Doug stood up from the table and walked to the door of the dining room. "You wait with Mummy, baby. I'll go and check your bed, OK?" he said with a heartwarming smile, nodding at his daughter.

Ivy smiled back at her father with a look of relief. *Daddy will scare away Tabitha,* she thought.

Doug walked across the bottom-floor hallway that led back to the study-slash-reception room. From the hall, oak staircase rose to a second landing that had two stands, each bearing a vase with dead flowers. Doug looked at the vases. *I better throw those flowers out tomorrow,* he thought. He climbed the staircase, finally reaching the second floor of the house.

The center of the second floor did not exist. It had no floor, with an open view of the floor below. A wooden banister ran all the way along the upstairs hallway, preventing persons from falling down onto the staircase below. There were two main bedrooms within the house: the master bedroom, where Doug and Joanne were going to be sleeping, and the children's room,

The House

which was located on the far left end of the landing. The floor that led to the rooms was crafted out of beechwood laminate. At the far right corner, there was a set of double doors leading to the balcony. The balcony overlooked the entire front and side lawn, with a view of the lake in the distance.

Also in the corner of the landing, by the double doors, was an old-fashioned rocking chair, one similar to what Doug had when he was a child. Upon the rocking chair were a number of dolls that had been left behind by who he assumed were the previous owners. South of the children's bedroom ran the rest of the landing, leading to the third small guest room and the main bathroom. Doug walked over to the children's bedroom and placed his hand on the door. He jumped back slightly. The doorknob was cold to the touch. He continued to open the door and walked into the room.

The room was the second-largest room on the second floor. It had the usual rectangle shape, with pink wallpaper the previous owners must have also used this as a children's bedroom, it seemed. Within the room were two metal-framework single beds. Each bed had a different duvet set upon it. Raine's had a Disney princess duvet set with characters from the film *Frozen*. Ivy's bed featured characters from *Finding Nemo*, which was her favorite Disney film.

Doug walked toward Ivy's bed. The room had a chill to it. He could see his own breath in front of him as he exhaled. A sharp chill slowly slithered its way down his back. He had the strange feeling that someone or something was watching him intently. He scanned the room, which was empty. He shrugged his shoulders, shaking off the unnerving feeling, and continued toward the bed. He pulled the cover away from the bed to reveal an empty bed and clean sheet. There was nothing in sight. He chuckled to himself. *My baby girl was imagining things,* he thought to himself, replacing the cover and tidying up the ends. As he began to walk away from the bed, in the corner of his eye he noticed a strange figure sitting on his other daughter's bed. He stopped dead in his tracks. The room went cold again. His breathing slowed right down in an instant. He could hear his own heart beating.

He turned slowly to face Raine's bed. He let out a massive sigh of relief. Sitting on the bed, with an ear-to-ear grin, was a doll. It was a strange-looking doll, granted, but it was a doll nonetheless. It had jet-black curly hair. It looked to be female, with a strange Victorian-style dress on. Its face was made of a well-worn fabric. It appeared to be old. Its eyes were as red as the sun setting on the eastern horizon.

He walked to the bed and picked up the doll by its waist, closely inspecting it. It seemed to be a normal doll, just with a strange look to it, especially the eyes. He then noticed a tag hanging from the doll's leg. Upon the tag was the name Tabitha. "Ah, you're Tabitha," he said to the doll, chuckling to himself. "Well, you leave my daughter Ivy alone. This is her room, not yours." He pointed at the doll mockingly as he pretended to be telling it off. He threw the doll back onto the bed and headed back to the dining room.

Doug strolled back into the dining room with a large smile on his face. "Tabitha is a doll the girls have found in their room," he said to Joanne with a laughing smile. He

The House

lifted Ivy up in his arms and cuddled her tightly. "Baby girl, Tabitha is just a doll. She's not going to hurt you."

Ivy looked up at him with adoring eyes. "Thanks, Daddy. I love you," she said with a weak smile.

"Daddy loves you too, baby girl." He placed her down again and began to clear the dining table of the empty plates.

After supper Joanne walked Raine and Ivy upstairs to bed leaving Doug to clear the dining room of all the plates and dirty glasses. Doug then retired to bed where Joanne was already lying down. It was a large and warm-feeling room, with the walls painted a bright yellow, a shade similar to a daffodil. The best part about the room was the Victorian four-poster bed they got to sleep on. It had a large, thick mattress that they could bounce up and down on like a child's air-filled bounce castle. The room also had access to the balcony via a set of pearl-white double doors, and at the far right end of the room, a doorway led to the en suite toilet.

He changed into his nightwear, which consisted of only a pair of blue-and-gray-checkered pajama bottoms. He dragged himself into bed and cuddled his wife, who lay on her side, facing the far wall. She looked over her shoulder with a smile of love upon her pale-skinned face. "I love you, baby," she said quietly.

Doug smiled back and kissed her passionately. "I love you more," he replied, kissing her on the back of the neck. The two parents fell to sleep quickly that night. It is doubtful they would have slept so easily knowing what was in store for them over the next few weeks!

2

The days began to wane, the nights closed in earlier, and the trees donned their vibrant hues. There was a chill that crept into the air-not the bite of winter, but just a nip to let them know there was a new season at hand. The rays of the sun cut through the thin, gray clouds like a stained glass window. Soon the fall leaves were stripped away, leaving the trees naked and cold. The grounds were colored scarlet and gold as the last life of the leaves escaped their veins. Autumn was upon Llyn Alwen.

Doug awoke from his sleep; it had been three weeks since they had moved into their new home. They were still in the middle of renovations. However, Doug had been doing all of the work. He had put up shelving in the girls' room, and he had fixed the downstairs toilet. He had also done the job of replacing the wallpapering in the downstairs hallway had also been done by him, leaving it a vibrant blue and cream. Doug was exhausted, and he had slept well that night.

He dragged himself out of bed, thrusting himself into his "old granddad" slippers, as he called them. Pulling himself upward, he continued to the door and exited onto the

The House

landing. He entered the downstairs study and looked at the old oak grandfather clock. It was 11:30 a.m. He clicked his neck, as he did most mornings, and continued into the kitchen. Joanne was already up and had left him a note on the gray marble kitchen counter. The kitchen was old style. It had a large island with an integrated sink. The pots and pans hung from the ceiling, held up by small cast-iron hooks like dead meat hanging in the freezer. The walls were painted a dark cream color, and the flooring was made from light-colored beechwood. Doug picked up the note that his wife had left him and began to read.

> *Doug, I didn't want to wake you. I know you've been tired. There are no jobs outstanding to be done at the house, you'll be glad to hear. Can you please pick up the girls from school at three o'clock? And I'll see you tonight when I get home.*
> *Love you millions. XXXXXXXX*

Doug chuckled to himself and placed the note back down on the worktop. He walked out of the kitchen and back into the study. The main armchair in the study was a comfy chair to sit in. Many times in the last few weeks, Doug would sit in this chair to relax and let the day's stress leak away from his body, cleansing him and renewing his inner peace. Today, however, he didn't need to de-stress and fancied a difference in seating. He wandered through the downstairs, considering the different options, but decided that none were to his liking that day. It then clicked. He marched his way back out of the study, down the hallway, and toward the front door. He let himself out into the crisp, bitter air. Turning to his left, he saw the beech rocking chair that had been left behind by the previous owners.

As he sat in the chair, it rocked backward violently, taking him by surprise. However, in time he got used to rocking it gently back and forth, back and forth. It reminded him of being on a seesaw with his kids, which he often did when taking the girls to the park. The air was thin, with a slight cold bite to it. "The summer is over," he said to himself, gazing across the lake. There was not a ripple in sight. The lake was like a rounded mirror with strange angles and sides, reflecting the thin, mucky-looking sky.

"I could look at this view for hours," he said, shuffling himself further into comfort while rocking back. Twenty minutes passed by before Doug reopened his eyes. He hadn't realized that he had dozed off. Shaking the feeling of tiredness, he stood up and walked back into the house. While walking down the hallway, he noticed something that made him stop dead in his tracks. Upon the wall, there was a picture that Doug had removed some days ago. It was the picture that he noticed on the first day they moved in.

The picture that he had put up in its place was nowhere to be seen. This picture, however, had been hung up neatly, just the way it had been when Doug had removed it. He scratched his head, most puzzled. *Maybe Joanne had moved the photo and put this one back up,* he thought. He shook his

The House

head, knowing that Joanne would not have replaced their family photo with a picture of a family they had never met. Feeling even more puzzled, he continued toward the staircase and began the climb to the upper level of the house.

Thinking it might be good to get out of the house, Doug decided to take a walk around the lake. He had read online that there were some amazing walking routes around the lake. With that in mind, he pulled on his gray cargo pants and his bottle-blue soft-shell outdoor jacket. He then put on a woolly hat and began his descent back downstairs. He left the house and began to walk down the path, which was buried beneath the dead leaves.

The track he had taken was a long dirt road with a strip of grass splitting the track into two. The naked trees towered high above him, standing close together like an army in tight formation. The wind swept through the trees, causing a low whistle to glide through the air. The wind slapped Doug in the face as if it were trying to antagonize him. The track went on for a mile or so before leading to a medium-length grassy trail.

Alongside the trail was a ten-foot drop, which would have positioned anyone who was to not notice it for a nasty fall to the jagged rocks below. The lake was in full view from the trail above. The wind had picked up slightly, causing the lake to stir. Small waves began to lift from the surface like charging bulls. The wind grew stronger and threw itself onto the surface, causing large ripples, as if God was casting large boulders into the lake. Doug continued to battle his way through the wind, which was now getting more intense.

Before him he could see a large section of dense woodland. "It will get me out of the wind, I guess," he said as he pushed his way against the wind, breaking into a fast-paced run toward the tree line. This section of the wooded area still had leaves upon the trees, causing the forest to appear dark and gloomy. The air was thin within the forest, due to the density of the leaves, and the atmosphere was cold and confined. Doug shivered as the cold chill crept down his spine like a serpent. He did not like this place. He debated turning back, looking behind him. However, the wind had now been joined by the rain, which cascaded down to the earth.

Doug sighed deeply and took in a deep breath. He turned back to face the dark woodland before him. Soon, however, after navigating his way through the trees for ten minutes or so, he began to feel less and less nervous and cold. Doug continued down the dirt track, looking into the distance and scanning his surroundings. He sensed that he was not the only person within these woods. The sound of soft footsteps could be heard eerily in the blowing wind.

A black wisp of clothing glided across the trees to the left of him. Doug turned to that direction, squinting. Nothing. *These woods are making me crazy,* he thought to himself as he continued deeper and deeper into the woods. "There!" he shouted aloud. There was a figure in the distance, hunched over, slowly walking toward him. As the figure drew closer, it came more into focus.

The fabric he had seen was a black woolen cloak. The figure was hooded, and the face underneath was riddled

The House

with wrinkles. The face of the woman beneath the hood was old, and time had not been kind to her. Strings of pearl-white hair dangled out from beneath the hood like tinsel in a Christmas tree. She continued toward Doug, holding a wooden walking stick with the head of a crow at the top. She was a very creepy-looking lady. She wore big, round glasses, which enlarged her dull-gray eyes, turning them into two moons. Her lips were thin, and a rather large tooth could be seen protruding from her mouth. She looked rather like a disfigured saber-toothed tiger.

Doug looked at her, intrigued by her appearance. She looked back, as she was only a few feet away from him now. She seemed surprised, as if she had never come across another person in these woods before. She looked him up and down as if she were sizing him up, and then came closer to investigate. "Hello," Doug said sharply, trying to begin a conversation with her. She stopped dead in her tracks and looked him squarely in the face.

"Hello, Doug," she said, with a blank face tilted to the side like a bird.

Doug's heart sank in his chest. "How do you know my name?"

The old woman began to cough a coarse, gruff cough, as if she smoked a hundred cigarettes daily. However, her coughing turned into an eerie chuckle. "I make it my business to know persons moving into the area," she replied. "I know your wife is called Joanne, and you have two lovely children, Ivy and Raine."

Doug continued to stare in bewilderment, his voice straining to leave his mouth.

"Doug, your estate agent told me about you," the old woman said with a thin grin stretching across her aged face.

"My estate agent," he repeated, thinking carefully back to the young girl who showed Doug and Joanne around the house only a month and a half ago. He thought back to when he drove down the rocky pathway toward the house. He had seen a slender young girl standing at the front of the house holding a black leather clipboard. Doug remembered her very well. She had been wearing a thin thigh-length skirt and a white blouse open to the bosom, her shoulder-length hazel-colored hair flowing down in curls. She had amazingly green eyes glinting like emeralds in the sun. Doug's mind began to wander thinking about that day.

A twig snapped in the distance, bringing Doug to the present. The elderly woman still stood in front of him, still looking him up and down. "Why would the estate agent tell you about me and my family?" he said looking at the lady again.

"Because I asked her. I was interested to know who was moving in."

Doug moved backward a couple of steps away from the lady.

"I don't understand."

"Let me introduce myself," she began as she removed her glasses. "My name is Belinda Black. I live within these woods. I have a house on the east shore of the lake."

The House

Doug continued to look confused.

"And I'm most pleased that I got to speak to you before it was too late."

This conversation was starting to go downhill and began to give Doug a nervous feeling. "I think it's best I be going now, Miss Black."

"Doug, I suggest you hear me out it's about the house you are living in," Belinda began to say as Doug started to fidget away from her, as a person slowly moves away from a viper that is ready to strike. "You and your family need to leave. Now!"

Doug stopped on the spot, and his fear and bewilderment now turned to anger. He stopped moving away and began to move forward toward the old, fragile woman. She saw his advance but did not flinch. "Who the hell do you think you are, coming to me threatening me and my family?" Doug said, clenching his fists tightly.

"I do not threaten. I merely say that house you are living in is dangerous," Belinda whispered, looking at Doug with sincerity.

Doug stopped advancing toward her, and his anger turned back to fear, his breath rising from his body into the air. "That house is my home. How is it dangerous?"

"That house has demons, demons that won't rest until your family suffers," Belinda uttered. "I have told people in the past, and they did not listen. Look what happened to them." Belinda moved her walking stick forward and began to skulk away into the dark forest.

"Wait what happened to the other families?" Doug shouted after her.

The elderly woman stopped by a large oak tree and slowly turned her head back to face Doug. A wisp of an evil smile came across her face. "She will come for you, Doug, if you don't get out." She smiled. "She will kill you all." With that, she turned back and disappeared into the thick wood.

His hairs stood up on the back of his neck. The trees began whispering those very words Belinda had just uttered: "She will kill you all." The woman's laugh rang in his ears.

She's crazy, absolutely crazy.

3

Doug couldn't shake off the unnerved feeling as he rumbled through the woods, the twigs snapping beneath his feet and the dead leaves crunching. The wind had died off now, and the forest was silent again. The rain had also stopped falling from the heavens. Beads of rain dripped off the trees in symphony with one another.

"She will kill you." Those words continued to echo in his mind; he could not shake the feeling of unease. Belinda Black was clearly mad, and Doug had the misfortune of meeting her in her natural habitat. And that stupid estate agent why had she given out his name to this crazy woman? Doug had a mind to contact the agency and raise a complaint.

A glimpse of light cut through the tree line, appearing to be leading Doug out of the crushing woods. With every step he took, he could see more and more sunrays visible through the canopy. He came to the end of the tree line and could see the lake in front of him. The dam could be seen from this viewpoint.

A gravity-arch masonry dam lying below a large water treatment facility was introduced with a cast-iron aqueduct laid beneath the ground, leading to Birkenhead. The dam had stood there for some time, being built back in 1909. It had begun to age and was built up with moss, which had begun poisoning the cracks in the stonework.

Doug could see his house in the distance behind the large tower that was located in the center of the dam. He began a fast-paced walk toward the dam, wanting to get clear of the woods and back to what he thought was safety. The grass was damp from the rain that had retreated back into the clouds. Small spiderwebs stretching between the grass stems caught tiny midge flies; the grass was riddled with these miniature gravesites.

He reached the foot of the tower and felt a hint of warm air soothe his body. *I'm safe,* he thought. He looked around to make sure his thought was a correct one. To the left of him, a set of masonry steps led to a platform that overlooked the lake. He walked up the steps, resting his arms on the stone wall. He was looking across the river when he saw the bewildering sight of a figure in the distance holding a walking stick and standing upon a large rock, on the far west shoreline of the lake. She was pointing directly at Doug. How she could see him, he did not know. A sudden cackling laugh could be heard echoing across the surface of the lake.

Doug stood dumbfounded at the sight. "She is one hundred percent barmy," he said out loud. He no longer semi-believed her tale about the house. She was clearly a very unwell, unstable woman. He chuckled to himself, not really understanding how he had let an old woman like Belinda

The House

Black convince him there was something wrong and that his family was in danger, and that his house had demons within. It suddenly hit him. He pulled his iPhone 6 with its dark, space-gray case out of his pocket and looked at the time stamp flashing on the screen.

It was 2:15. "Shit, the girls," he said, slapping his forehead. He had to be in the small town of Denbigh in thirty minutes' time to pick the girls up from school. Doug left the platform and broke into a run toward the house. He ripped the door of his Volvo open and jumped into the driver's seat. The engine roared to life. He placed the car into gear and set off.

Denbigh, a small market town with a population off 9,876, was a very close-knit community. The town had grown from nothing during the glove industry era. It was granted its borough charter back in the twelfth century. At that point the town was still housed within the town walls. The town was involved in the AD 1294-1295 revolt of Madog ap Llywelyn, in which the castle was captured in the autumn, and the forces were defeated by the Welsh rebellion. The town was eventually recaptured by Edward the First. Denbigh was home to many Welsh revolts, one famous one being the revolt of Owain Glyndwr, in which the town was burned, in AD 1400.

Now Denbigh was a simple town with shops and cafés where the elderly population would sit and discuss times long since gone. Denbigh was also home to numerous public houses, where many of the male community hung around to laugh and joke with their closest friends, play darts, and watch the football matches being streamed live on the televisions.

Denbigh had one primary school, located on the outskirts of the town. It was a large cobblestoned building with a bell tower. The bell was now decommissioned due to health and safety regulations; however, many of the children's parents and their parents remembered the bell being rung when it was lunchtime at school or time to go home.

The school's play area was the size of a football field, with various parklike attractions. Doug drove into the main lot of the school at a quarter to three on the dot. He heaved a large sigh of relief. "Made it," he said with a chuckle. As he exited the vehicle, the sound of the children laughing in the playground could be heard in the lot. Their happy laughs rang through the air.

Doug moved to the cast-iron gate that led to the playground. There were hundreds of children, ranging from four to eleven years old, running around like headless chickens, screaming and laughing as they played. As he scanned the crowd, he saw Ivy sitting on her own at the far end of the playground. Raine suddenly appeared next to him, out of breath.

"Hi, Daddy," she said, jumping into his arms. He kissed her on the cheek and squeezed her tightly with affection. As he placed her back on the ground, he looked back at Ivy, who was still sitting on the small bench. Doug started to navigate the crowd of children, wading through them like waves hitting the coastal shorelines.

"Mr. Moore," a female voice called from the distance. Doug steered his attention to the voice, homing in on Mrs. Harriet Fysh, Ivy's schoolteacher. She wore half-moon rimmed glasses and had a soft, gentle complexion. Her black hair was neatly tied into a bun and reflected the light.

The House

"Mrs. Fysh," he replied, extending his hand to greet her.

She shook it and continued. "I need to speak to you about Ivy. It's rather important we speak now." She looked concerned.

Doug turned to Raine, who was still behind him. "Princess, why don't you go and get your sister so we can go home, OK?" he said with a cheeky wink. She smiled and began to walk toward Ivy, who still sat in the distance.

He turned his attention back to Mrs. Fysh. "How can I help, Mrs. Fysh?"

"Well, it's about Ivy. How has she been behaving at home since the move here?"

He looked at her blankly. "She has been fine better than I expected. Why do you ask?"

She cleared her throat. "Well, in school today, she has been crying to a member of the staff."

"What all day? Why wasn't I informed?" he replied, a hint of anger in his voice.

Mrs. Fysh, sensing this displeasure, put her hands up in front of her chest. "Mr. Moore, she has only been crying for the last hour. However, she has disclosed some rather disturbing comments."

Doug began to feel nervous now. "What kind of comments?"

"Well, she has told us that there is a girl called Tabitha living with you at your house. And that she has been telling her nasty things, such as to make her go away."

Doug sighed with relief, thinking that he was going to be accused of some sort of mistreatment.

Mrs. Fysh looked at him sternly. "Mr. Moore, I don't think you are grasping the gravity of this."

"Mrs. Fysh, let me explain," Doug said, waving his hands. "Tabitha is a doll that was left at the house we have just moved into; she is completely harmless."

Mrs. Fysh still looked concerned at this news.

"What is it, Mrs. Fysh?" Doug asked.

She cleared her throat again. "Well, Ivy has told me something a little more disturbing than just that."

Doug again started to feel concerned.

"This Tabitha has also told Ivy that she is going to make her dead."

The only word that Doug heard out of the whole sentence that had just left her lips was "dead." That word rang in his mind for a short moment. He then looked at Mrs. Fysh again.

"She has told us that Tabitha says this in her dreams and that she has bad dreams."

"I don't understand Tabitha is a doll," Doug squeaked.

Mrs. Fysh moved closer to Doug as if to whisper something to him. "Mr. Moore, I really think Ivy may need to see someone about her feelings."

"Let me speak with my wife; she needs to be involved in this."

Mrs. Fysh nodded in agreement. "Let me know how things go."

Doug smiled weakly at Mrs. Fysh and walked over to his children. He picked up Ivy and held her tightly. "Are you ok,

The House

sweetheart?" he said, noticing a tear on her cheek and wiping it away. She turned to look at him, her face pale, as if she had seen a ghost. She shook her head, not speaking.

He walked over to the car and put the children in the backseat. As he strapped Ivy into her seat, she grabbed her father's arm tightly. "Daddy, can I sleep with you and Mummy tonight?" Her eyes teared up again.

He smiled at her, trying to make her smile. "Of course, sweetheart, you can sleep with Mummy and Daddy tonight."

Her face began to lighten up, and that cute smile began to form.

Doug winked at Ivy, got into the driver's seat, and began driving away from the school. The drive home was long, and not much was said. Ivy did not speak a word. Raine was telling her father about her day and that she had gotten a gold star for her homework. He was happy that Raine was doing well in her new school.

As they drove down the driveway toward the house, Doug could see the figure of his wife waiting on the porch for her family to arrive. The children climbed out of the car. Raine ran to the house to greet her mother, showing her the gold star. Ivy, on the other hand, stood by the car, facing the woodland behind the house. Doug watched his daughter for a short moment.

Ivy's face went pale, the blood draining from it. Her eyes widened as she stared at the woods. At one point she looked as though the woods had possessed her and taken hold of her.

"Ivy," he shouted. She did not make any movement; she did not even appear to have heard him. He slowly moved toward her; the wind was picking up.

He placed his hand on her shoulders and leaned in. Ivy's breathing was slow and cold. "Ivy, what's wrong?" Doug asked.

Her eyes began to well and tear up again, her cheeks twitching violently. "She…she can see me." Her face exploded with fear as she let out a scream of pain.

Ivy fell to the ground, wriggling around like a worm exposed from the earth. Her screaming was ear piercing and heart stabbing.

Doug grabbed his screaming child and pulled her close to him. "Ivy, it's ok, it's ok. Daddy's got you," he said, running his hand repeatedly across her hair as he tried to calm her down.

"She's hurting me, Daddy. She's hurting me!" she screeched as her eyes squeezed closed.

With one last violent jerk of the body, she stopped screaming. Her body now quivered like a leaf in spring winds. Her eyes glazed, looking into space. Doug waved his hand in front of her face, clicking his fingers and trying to bring her to reality. At this point Joanne was standing above them, looking down on her daughter lying in her father's arms.

Ivy's eyes began to blink, and she started to look around. Her father's face came into view. Her lower lip trembled with fear. Doug brought her to her feet, still holding her arms to balance her. Joanne knelt down, grabbing hold of Ivy around

The House

the waist, hugging her tightly. "Darling, what happened?" she cried, with tears streaming down her face. Doug looked around and saw Raine standing on the porch, with the fear of what she had just seen clear on her face.

"She h-h-hurt me, M-m-u-mmy," she stuttered. "She saw me and s-s-h-e hurt me."

Joanne wiped her own tears away from her cheeks.

"Who hurt you, baby girl?" Doug said, looking even more concerned.

With a slow reply, she whispered the name Doug did not want to hear.

"Tabitha."

4

Joanne was normally a very calm and collected person. She had to be, as she had given birth to two children in the last couple of years, and she had a husband who had just had gone through being an alcoholic. "The incident" was what made her calm and well collected.

She had to take control of the incident and get her and her husband through it. Nothing, however, could have prepared her for today's events. She had just seen her daughter lying on the ground in Doug's arms screaming her little heart out and shaking uncontrollably.

Joanne had taken Ivy to their bed, as Ivy had asked Doug earlier. She changed her into her pajamas and tucked her snugly into the bed. She turned on the television raised upon the wall in front of the bed, putting on Ivy's favorite children's program to console her.

She left the room, making her way into the children's bedroom. The doll, Tabitha, sat on Raine's bedside chair where all her other teddies and dolls sat. She walked to the chair, grasped the doll in her hands tightly, and left the room.

The House

Raine stood at the bottom of the stairs, staring up at her. "Mummy, what are you doing with Tabitha?" she asked quietly.

"Why, poppet, this is not your doll, is it?"

"She was left here, Mummy. She's cute. I like her," she replied. "She was abandoned, and I am taking care of her."

"We will talk about this later, Raine; I need to speak to your father," she said, walking toward the kitchen. Doug stood staring out of the kitchen patio window. The sun was setting on the western horizon. Joanne stepped into the room. Doug, noticing her presence, turned to face her. His face was drowned in fear and upset.

"What are we going to do?" he mumbled, walking toward the kitchen island. Joanne took a breath and placed the doll on the table. Doug looked at the doll with a face of thunder. "Where did you find that thing?" he growled. Joanne turned to him with a stern look. He backed down immediately.

"This doll is not the cause of this," Joanne roared across at him. "The cause of this problem is us, our past, and the changes we have put her through."

Doug knew where this conversation was going. "So basically you are blaming me for this," he said, looking down at the floor in disbelief.

Joanne slammed her fist against the kitchen countertop. "Did I say I was blaming you, Doug?" she screamed, her fists still clenched. "I was merely saying that all the changes in our lives have clearly upset Ivy."

Doug moved toward Joanne in a swift motion. "Listen, Joanne, the main thing we need to do is make sure Ivy is safe, and that thing," he said, pointing in the doll's direction, "is gone out of this house!"

"And what do you suggest we do with it?" Joanne replied.

"We could burn it in the outside fire burner," Doug said, looking out to the front lawn.

Joanne looked horrified at the idea. "We can't just burn the thing. What if the old owners come back for it?"

Doug laughed at this, looking at Joanne aggressively. "I don't care if they come back here. They shouldn't have left the damn thing here," he thundered.

Joanne grabbed the doll, holding her tightly to her chest. "Raine has fallen in love with the doll. We can't just throw her away."

Doug looked up sharply. "What do you mean Raine has fallen in love with it?"

"She told me that she was taking care of her because the old owners had abandoned her here."

Doug moved closer to Joanne now; their faces were nearly touching. "That thing is going. No more arguments. Give it here, please," Doug said, putting out his hand.

Joanne gave him a vicious look. "If you burn this doll, so help me, there will be trouble," she rumbled, her eyes wide and alert.

Doug snatched the doll from her clutches and stormed out of the house.

The House

Joanne pursued him, walking out into the courtyard. However, instead of going to the log burner, Doug threw the car door open and started the engine. Joanne ran to the car window, hammering on the pane of glass.

Doug opened his window a small amount to speak to her. "I'm taking the doll away from here, Joanne. I'm doing this for our daughter's sake. Please understand," he said, his eyes welling up with concern.

Without another word, he was gone, hurtling toward the pathway to the main road. Joanne felt, for the first time in a long time, a sense of terror and worry as the sun set beyond the hills.

5

Doug's mind was focused on only one thing: getting rid of this stupid doll! His car rocketed along the country lanes, weaving in and out of the bends like a large serpent. His mind was racing faster than ever before. His two inner voices argued over the fact of him taking the doll. "This doll needs to go. It's hurting Ivy," his good inner voice shouted from within.

"Don't be stupid. Dolls don't hurt people. It's all in her imagination," the other voice countered.

"Shut up, the two of you," Doug snapped and slammed his foot on the accelerator. The car pushed harder and faster along the road.

It was dark now. The road surface glinted from the rays of moonlight from above. The trees on either side of the road rose high into the heavens. In the distance he saw a sign with a finger pointing down a small tarmac road marking the entrance to Llyn Brenig. *Perfect. I'll dispose of the doll here,* he thought.

He turned onto the small road, which slowly descended into a small parking lot. The reservoir began to emerge in the

The House

distance. The water was black in the dim light. The wind was only slight, and the surface was still, not a swell in sight.

Doug pulled up in the lot, where the road came to an end. He exited his car and pulled the doll from the passenger side. The wind began to pick up. A haze of mist began to rise from the hills above, rolling down the hillside like a white avalanche toward the lake below. The air was cold, burning his nostrils.

His nose and ears began to redden as the blood rushed to warm them. Doug could feel his heart pumping furiously within his ribcage, like an angry tiger trying to escape its capturers. A pathway led from the lot toward the lake itself.

The walk was not long; it was about half a mile to the lake's shores. "Tabitha," he said, looking at the doll as he walked, his icy-cold fingers clenched around her waist, "I am doing this for my child. I hope you understand that." He looked into those small red eyes as he spoke.

"What the hell are you saying, man," his inner voice said. "It's a doll it's not a person." Doug shook his head, trying to clear the voice away. The trees began to waver as the wind roared. Certain trees appeared to be buckling under the strain from the wind, and almost seemed to be falling.

The lake's shoreline came into view. The murky, black water crashed against the pebble beachhead. Swells had begun forming in the lake rising high above Doug's height and wailing as they came crashing down. Doug looked above into the heavens. God was displeased with today's events, it appeared.

The clear sky had now been replaced with a dark canopy. The clouds were as black as the night.

Rain began to fall, gentle at first, like a child's tears. However, before long, the rain began to lash down, cutting into the earth and churning it up. The rain was beating Doug in the face, slicing into him.

Doug saw the walkway to the beachhead, a long, beech-pallet walkway with a small platform at the end. He stood at the end of the walkway, looking out to the lake, which was now a battlefield in itself. The waves had grown larger still, hitting into one another and trying to knock the others down.

Part of Doug wanted to leave the doll where he stood. However, he knew he had to do this properly. He began to move across the walkway. It was unstable in parts. The wood creaked below him as he walked. The waves crashed into the side of the walkway. Doug held onto the wooden railings for dear life.

Without warning, a freakishly large wave rose from the depths, rising to the size of a two-story house. It crashed into the walkway, lifting Doug off his feet and throwing him over the side, with the doll cast onto the walkway.

Doug was now overboard, in the lake itself. The water was trying to drag him downward, attempting to drown him. He held onto the side of the walkway, still refusing to let go and looking around frantically for something to help him pull himself out of the water.

He had the chilling feeling that something was lurking in the depths. There was no time for seeing things. Above him he

The House

a saw a thick bit of sailing rope attached to one of the posts of the causeway. He threw out his arm in an attempt to grab it. With every inch closer he got, it seemed to move farther away.

The darkness of death began to close in. The breath in his lungs slowly faded away. The last few weeks' events flashed before his eyes. Suddenly the rope was lowered from above, as if someone was on the causeway. He tried to look through glazed eyes; the lack of air affected his vision. There was a dark silhouette above him. He did not recognize it. He felt the roughness feel of the rope in his hands and pulled himself upward.

As he emerged from the water, he took in a large gulp of air. He pulled himself onto the causeway and lay there coughing his guts up. His heart raged as his lungs grasped every bit of air they could. Recovering a bit, he lifted himself to his feet.

He scanned the causeway. The figure was nowhere to be seen. He looked around for the doll, which had also disappeared from sight. *Must have fallen in to the lake with the wave,* he thought. Doug was drenched to the bone. Water leaked through his clothes like ink on parchment.

The wind was still heavy, battering the causeway. Doug could feel it rocking to and fro in the wind. The only source of light came from the small lantern hanging from one of the posts. This, however, the lighting was short lived. A gust of wind threw the lantern into the air; it was swallowed within the dark abyss below.

Then the unexpected, violent sound of wood being ripped tore Doug's attention from the drowned light. He turned to find the wooden planks of the causeway behind him being ripped from the structure, flying into the air above. The waves were viciously attacking the causeway as if to collapse it. The waves were succeeding.

Without another thought, Doug ran for the shore. His legs burned with pain as he ran for safety. From above, a plank of wood came toward him, seemingly aiming for his head. The plank narrowly missed, crashing onto the causeway. With only a few more steps in front of him, he leaped to shore. He landed hard on the pebble beach, with a spray of stones spewing up in his face.

The causeway buckled under the pressure of the galling winds, and with a large crash, the end of the structure collapsed into the lake below. Shortly after, the whole causeway sank into the black hole. The lake devoured it whole. *Someone is out to get me,* Doug said to himself as he looked to the heavens.

Doug got to his feet and regained his breath. Brushing himself off, he began his walk back to the car. The wind had died down to just a breeze. The clouds above, however, were still dark. Doug looked down at his hand, which seared with pain. Blood oozed from a large gash across his palm.

When he reached the car, he walked to the back. He opened the trunk, and he dug out the bottle of vodka hidden beneath the spare. Doug poured it onto his hand. It burned with pain as the vodka sank into the wound. Doug could feel the urges begin to fester within. "Go on you deserve a drink," his inner voice whispered sweetly. "Especially after that experience."

The House

Doug could feel the beads of sweat gathering on his forehead. His lips began to quiver, and saliva was beginning to build within his mouth. The anticipation of the taste and longing grew too strong. Before he could stop himself, the rim of the bottle was on his lips. Without a breath, Doug guzzled the whole bottle.

The alcohol traveled to his brain, breaking the barrier, causing him to feel lightheaded. He felt unsteady on his feet, and his vision began to blur. He fell to his knees as calmness and warmth washed over his body, cleansing him. His inner voice was now quiet, no longer tempting him. The inner voice had won.

Doug was now at the mercy of the alcohol coursing through his blood. He lay back against the bodywork of the car, letting his mind wander. He began to daydream a vision of himself and his family on a large cruise ship.

Sailing the Atlantic Ocean, heading for the sweet, sunny Caribbean. Raine and Ivy playing in the onboard swimming pool. Doug and Joanne sunbathing on the deck chairs. Doug holding a large cocktail in his hand. The sun beaming down on them from above.

Doug was brought quickly back to reality as his mobile phone began to chime in his pocket. Joanne was calling him. He gazed down through his drunken eyes. He had been gone for over two hours. Using all his capable strength, he pulled himself to his feet. Doug, at this point, was extremely intoxicated and could barely function, let alone drive.

However, he got into the car and into the driver's seat. He stabbed the key into the ignition. He made a few attempts to start the car; however, he failed miserably. Doug slammed his forehead into the steering wheel. With one last turn, the vehicle sprang to life. He slipped the car into reverse and left the lot.

Returning to the main road, he set out toward home, thinking of how he was going to hide his drunkenness from his wife. He looked at the road ahead. It was dark; the only light to be seen was that from his headlights. Doug's car began to sway from side to side as Doug faltered behind the wheel.

Doug's hands started to shake uncontrollably. A strange, unnerving feeling washed over him. The hairs on his neck tingled with alarm. Suddenly, at the side of his car, an elderly woman emerged from the tree line. Doug was only a few feet from her. There was nothing he could do; she was too close for him to react.

There was a large thump, and the woman went flying forward. Doug slammed on the brakes, stammering, not knowing what to do. His past came rushing back "The incident" was happening all over again. Doug's body quivered. He was unable to control it.

He looked out at the body of the old woman. She was face down on the tarmac. She was wearing a pale-gray dress with frilly seams. Her long gray hair seeped from her head like tree trunks in the tarmac. Doug exited his car and slowly walked toward the lady.

The House

The drunken state quickly drained from his body, replaced by the feeling of sheer panic. "Hello, are you ok?" Doug shouted. There was no response. The fear hit him even harder now. *Was she dead?* he wondered.

He knelt down and reached out his hand. Suddenly the old woman sat upright. Doug jumped backward in horror at the sight in front of him. The woman slowly turned her head to face him. And what he saw was the most horrifying thing he had ever seen.

His hairs leaped from his skin in fear. A chill shot down his spine. The woman's face was old, older than Belinda Black's. Large wrinkles surrounded her cheeks and forehead. The horrifying feature, however, was not her face, but her eyes.

There were no eyes! Her eye sockets were exposed and vacant, showing no signs of life. They were dark within, just black and dead looking. They were jagged around the edges, as if her eyes had been cut out from her face. Her mouth appeared to be sewn shut. She was unable to open her mouth.

Her head tilted as if she knew of Doug's presence. "Oh my god who has done this to you?" he spluttered in fear. The lady's lips twitched as if she was trying to reply. Doug edged closer, and she reacted to his movement. She got to her feet, and Doug backed away from her. She threw her arms up, attempting to grab Doug. Doug ran to his car. She pursued him, running after him. Doug dived into his car, locking the doors. The woman threw her weight against the door. Nothing happened. She peered into the car with her empty sockets.

An eerie squeaking sound filled the car as she slowly rubbed her face against the window. She pulled her pale hands down the window slowly leaving deep smear marks. It looked like blood. She held up a finger to the window and began to write a message in the blood.

It chilled him to the very bone. "I'm coming for you." Doug let out a cry of fear. He threw the car into gear and sped off, leaving the woman standing in the road. He looked in his rearview mirror. The woman stood there, still waving at him as he drove away. He blinked once, and she vanished into thin air.

Doug did not stop. He continued to drive and did not look back. Finally, his house came into view. He pulled into courtyard. Doug stumbled of the car, looking up at the house.

"Where the hell have you been, Doug?" Joanne was at the door, her arms crossed in displeasure.

Leaving out most of the night's events, he pointed at the car. "Baby, someone has put a threatening message on the car window," Doug ranted.

She huffed and walked down to him, inspecting the glass. She sighed again. "Have you been drinking?" she said, smelling the strong odor of vodka on his breath.

Doug looked down at his shoes in shame after he saw the look on his wife's face. "I'm sorry, sweetheart. I'm trying my best. It's so hard after all that has been happening," he said, burying his face in his hands and weeping.

Joanne looked at her crying husband. Compassion overcame her. She pulled him into a tight, loving embrace. "Doug,

The House

we'll get there. It doesn't happen overnight," Joanne said. "But we will get there."

Doug looked up into her eyes and kissed her lovingly.

"Come on, let's go to bed," she said, grabbing his hand and leading him to the door. He turned to take a last look at the message on the window. To his horror, it was gone!

6

The morning sunrise put on a breathtaking show of radiant colors. Flares of red, pink, and orange scared away the dark blue and purple of the twilight sky. The new colors blended together like a prism.

The sun peeked over the mountains on the east horizon, its beautiful rays already shining brightly, warming the air from the cold, miserable air of the night before. The orchestra of early morning chirping echoed through the air, filling it with song and happiness.

Doug stood mesmerized at the beautiful display Mother Nature was putting on for him. The glistening reflections of the sun on the lake's surface made a feeling of awe sweep over him, warming his blood.

But last night's events still haunted his inner mind's eye. The horrifying sight of that woman's face the dead eyes and that mouth with the close stitching keeping it shut. Doug shuddered. He placed his hand on the window frame to support himself.

From behind, Joanne entered the room. She was dressed for work in a sexy black cotton pencil skirt and a professional-looking,

The House

pure-white, open-collared blouse. She was wearing her distinctive Jimmy Choo Flash perfume. The aroma of pink pepper, tangerine, and strawberries ensnared his senses.

Doug's primal senses rose from the deep crevices of his body and took over. "Looking good, sexy," he said with a charming smile. He slowly moved toward her, like a wild panther stalking its prey. Joanne, noticing her husband's presence, smiled at him.

"Baby, there is no way I am undressing," she said, placing her hand on Doug's chest. "It's taken me an hour to get ready for work."

"Aww," Doug whined in disappointment, sitting back on the bed.

"What are you going to do today?"

Doug shrugged and stood up. "Not sure. Might do the garden, water the plants."

Joanne nodded in agreement. She left the room, her light footsteps disappearing down the stairs. Doug walked back to the window, his mind now returning back to last night, reliving it in his mind's eye.

He heard Joanne downstairs running to the staircase, then the sound of her bounding up the stairs toward the bedroom. The sound of distress was in the air! She threw open the door, breathing heavily like an out-of-breath pug.

Doug looked at her, concerned. "Babe, what's wrong?"

Still panting, she said, "Come quick, downstairs, quick!" she stuttered breathlessly.

"What is it?"

"Just come," she huffed, running back down the stairs. Doug followed after, his mind racing, dreading what he was going to find.

Coming to the bottom of the stairs, Doug jumped the last couple of steps, landing on the floor of the study. Doug now knew the source of his wife's distress. The study had been turned upside down. The bookcases were now bare, with thousands of books strewn across the floor.

The leather chairs were thrown against the walls. One chair was hanging from its legs on the wall. The family pictures and their frames were smashed on the floor and placed in a pile at the entrance to the hallway.

"What in the hell?" Doug was amazed by the large mess that had been made.

"That's not all," Joanne said, walking toward the kitchen. Doug followed her into the room. The kitchen was also a jungle of rubbish.

Paper towels hung from the ceiling, like vines within a tropical forest. The kitchen tap sprayed out water, which now covered the island and the surrounding floor. Pans had been thrown across the room, and smashed plates littered the island surface and the floor.

Doug waded through the lagoon forming on the floor and turned the tap off.

"I don't understand," Joanne said, shaking her head in disbelief.

"Me either," Doug replied, throwing tea towels on the floor and mopping up the water.

The House

"Why would someone do this?" Doug looked around the room. The scary image of an unknown intruder ransacking his house entered his mind. A sudden sense of fear ran through his nerves like the chill of an icy winter wind. He looked at Joanne.

"Joanne," he said with alarm as he rushed to the stairs, and bounded up them. He ripped open the girls' bedroom door. Raine screamed, startled, as she was getting ready for school. The room was normal no damage or mess. "Sorry, Princess, Daddy didn't mean to scare you."

Doug left the room, walking into his own. Ivy was fast asleep on Doug's side of the bed. She looked so peaceful, like a village cricket green on Sunday. She was holding her teddy bear close to her, with her thumb in her mouth, which was her comforting mechanism.

Joanne joined him, with Raine in tow. "I'm going to have to get Raine to school. I think Ivy should stay home today, especially after yesterday's events. I'm late; I've got to get going," she said, pulling on her coat. "We will talk about this later when I get home." Doug and she kissed, and she left with Raine at her side.

The morning passed quickly as Doug cleaned up the study, restocking the empty bookcases with the books from the floor. The cleaning frenzy carried on into the later morning, with continued checks on Ivy, who was still fast asleep in her parents' bed. He then continued his cleaning in the kitchen.

Cleaning the kitchen took him only forty minutes. He picked up the broken plates and placed the pans back on their hooks. Doug's attention was drawn to the kitchen island surface. He saw something that confused him beyond all understanding.

On the surface lay a picture. It was the family picture that was missing from the hallway. The frame was in good condition; inside, however, there was a strange alteration. The faces of Doug, Joanne, Raine, and Ivy had been cut out of the picture, leaving the bodies headless.

Doug lifted the picture and walked to the study. The images in his head were not making any sense. His mind went back to the previous night and to the image of a woman writing a horrifying message on the glass in blood. *Who is she?*

He rushed out the front door and down the stairway to his parked car. He bent down to inspect the front bumper for any signs of damage. To his horror, there was no sign of any damage, not even a scratch. Then, looking up at the window, he saw clean glass.

He stood up, shaking his head, trying to repress the memories. He could not talk to Joanne about this she would never believe him. Who would believe his story about an old woman with no eyes and a stitched-up mouth attacking him and threatening to come after him, after he hit her while drunk driving? It was ludicrous! *Maybe it wasn't real. It must have been the drink. That's the only explanation.*

Doug walked back to the garden stairway, sat down, and rested his head against his hands. *It must have been the drink,* he thought. But it had never happened before.

The House

Doug thought maybe it was the Lord himself giving him a sign, trying to steer him off the alcohol. However, a strange feeling was lurking in his deep unconscious mind. The events of that night felt real, and Doug could not shake off that feeling.

7

Joanne returned home early that evening. She had had a busy day at work, and she discussed her day all throughout dinner. After the meal was over, Joanne ordered the children to take a shower and brush their teeth-the usual routine before bed.

This was the first opportunity for the two to discuss the morning's atrocities. "I still cannot believe this morning," Joanne said, sipping hot tea while she sat on one of the armchairs.

"I know. You think we should call the police?"

Joanne placed her cup of tea on the oak coffee table. "No," Joanne said. "We don't need to involve them; we need to be more careful."

"What do you mean?"

"Well, we must have left the back door open, and an animal came in and messed up the house."

"An animal?" Doug said, confused.

"Yes, an animal. Most likely a badger or a fox," Joanne murmured.

Doug wasn't sure if he agreed with his wife's diagnosis of the morning. However, he did not want to argue with

The House

her. The two sat in silence, watching an evening program on the BBC. When the show ended, Doug headed upstairs and walked into the girls' room.

Raine was already in bed, cuddling one of her dolls and playing with its hair. Ivy, however, sat at the window, gazing out at the moonlit lake.

"You ok, baby girl?" Doug moved over to the window. He knelt down next to her, cuddling her from behind.

"I'm ok, Daddy," she said, turning to hug him. He held her firmly.

"Good," Doug said, kissing his daughter's head. He lifted her into his arms and carried her to her bed. He tucked her in tightly and kissed her once again on her forehead. "Goodnight, Ivy," Doug said, standing up.

He walked over to Raine, tucking her in. "Good night, Raine," he said, kissing her on the cheek.

"Good night, Daddy," the girls said in synchrony. Doug left the room and walked into his own. Joanne was lying on the bed wearing a black silk chemise, with dark black stockings rising up her smooth legs.

She had a look of mischief on her face. "Hello, baby. I've been waiting for you," she said, getting to her knees and crawling slowly to the end of the bed.

Doug felt butterflies stir in his plexus. His heart began to thump from the adrenaline coursing through his veins. The attraction of the sexual and physical act before him lured him in. The tactile, euphoric feeling in his skin rumbled down into his loins and kidneys as the arousal began. The prickling on the back of his neck headed south to the bottom point of his spine. His heart continued to beat in a wild frenzy. Euphoria clouded his judgment, ensnaring his senses. Eyes dropping, palms sweating, and lips twitching, he walked to the bed, taking his wife into his arms. He slowly kissed her, the heat of their entwined bodies burning like a thousand suns.

Four hours had passed, and Joanne, exhausted, lay asleep on the rug of hair on Doug's chest. Doug stroked the sensitive under part of Joanne's arm. The moonlight shone through the thin curtains, casting dancing shadows around the room. The quiet, peaceful night, however, freakishly changed. The rumbling of thunderclouds rolled into the valley, like legions of troops marching into battle.

The thunder god, Thor, shot lightning bolts from the sky, lashing out at everyone and everything in his path. His voice boomed like a nuclear bomb. Wind whipped the trees and the house. The howling of his frustrated voice fought to get through the roof to Doug and his family.

Doug sat up in bed. Rain had begun to fall, sheet after sheet of water crashing down against the bedroom window like waves and waves of machine gun fire. The wind banged against the walls of the house, shaking its foundations. The knobs on their bedroom doors shook under the pressure. The moon had now retreated behind the crowds of clouds smothering the sky, putting the room in darkness.

A scream rang out from somewhere outside the house. Doug's blood turned to ice. He threw off the covers and ran for the window. As he peered out the window, scanning the

The House

lawn below, he saw nothing, nothing but the rain lashing down on the ground. Small ponds of water formed in the potholes in the beaten track to the house.

The scream sounded throughout the house. It wasn't just any scream it was Ivy! Doug was in the girls' room in an instant. Raine was fast asleep; the storm hadn't woken her. Ivy's bed was empty. Doug lifted the covers, searching under the bed. Nothing. Doug, with a wave of panic, stood up and ran to the landing.

Doug's forehead was sweating. He saw Joanne running up the stairs. "Where is she?" she said, her fear growing.

Doug was ashen, filled with dread. "I don't know," he replied. Another scream then came, again sounding as if it were coming from outside. Doug ran down the stairs, throwing himself into the cold rain.

The screams continued, and Doug could now tell that they were coming from the woods near the house. "You stay in the house in case she comes back," Doug yelled to Joanne. He turned to face the dark woods in front of him. It was pitch black, with the only light coming from blasts of lightning, which briefly illuminated the sky like a floodlight.

Without another thought about the darkness in front of him or the icy-cold rain drenching his cotton pajama bottoms, Doug dashed into the woods. The tall trees were only a couple of feet apart. The canopy above seemed to drum as the rain bounced off the branches and the few remaining leaves. It was completely dark now. Doug could barely see a foot in front of himself.

The screams quaked through the forest. With each scream, it felt like he was getting closer to the source. "Ivy," he shouted, his voice echoing through the trees.

"Daddy, Daddy, help me," Ivy's voice shrieked, coming from somewhere nearby. A sudden beam of moonlight broke through the clouds, illuminating a group of trees in front of him. As he closed in, he noticed a small figure held against a tree, a small child. It looked like Ivy. He walked toward her; an unnatural aura surrounded the scene. Ivy was standing against the tree, not moving. As he drew closer to her, he noticed a rope around her, binding her to the tree.

"Oh my god," Doug yelled. "Ivy!" He ran to the tree and tried to untie Ivy, but the rope would not budge. He then looked at his daughter's face. It hit like a freight train. It wasn't Ivy tied to the tree it was another girl.

It was a girl of the same age as Ivy. However, she had black hair and was wearing an old-fashioned Victorian nightdress. Her head was limp, facing the ground. Doug lifted her head up and let out a cry of terror, nearly throwing up.

The young girl's eyes were lifeless. However, the stomach-turning thing was the girl's throat, which had been slit from end to end, a deep laceration exposing her windpipe within. Doug grabbed his mouth as a strong feeling of nausea washed over him.

To Doug's horror, she then awoke, gasping for air, like a fish out of water. "What happened to you?" Doug asked. With a look of confusion that then turned to anger, she looked at

The House

him, her eyes bleeding. With an ear-deafening scream, she lunged forward, wrestling with her bindings.

Doug fell backward into the hard tree trunk behind him. The girl still screamed at the top of her lungs. Doug closed his eyes tightly, wishing the sight away. The scream suddenly stopped. *I've gone deaf,* Doug thought.

He opened his eyes to find that the girl had disappeared. No trace. There was no rope, no blood nothing! The tree was just a tree. Doug, in a frenzy, got to his feet. The eerie whistle of the wind sounded through the forest. Another scream now came from the house.

Doug turned away from the tree, breaking into a sprint, dodging the trees. The long branches whipped his face as he ran. Ivy's screams were even higher pitched than before. *What the hell is going on,* Doug thought, and panic overtook him.

The house came into view, the lights from the windows shining in the surrounding darkness. Doug smashed through the front door like a fireman into a burning building. The house was cold like a subzero freezer. Condensation was growing on the windows and on the lamp glasses. Doug's blood was cold, running slowly through his body.

"Ivy, baby girl, where are you?" Doug screamed into the house.

"Daddy, I'm down here." Ivy's voice was coming from under the floorboards.

Underground, he thought. *How did she get down there?*

Doug ran into the kitchen, heading for the cellar door. The door was on the far side of the room. It was an old, dark, wooden door. Standing tall, Doug shivered slightly. It was a very creepy-looking door.

Doug noticed that a metal bar had been wedged against the door. Ivy's screams could be heard below. Doug threw the metal bar off the door, ripping it open. The hinges screamed in pain. The stone steps led into a dark abyss. He turned on the light for the cellar; however, no light appeared.

He grabbed a flashlight out of the side cupboard and sank into the darkness. The air was thin and cold, filled with a thick dust, which got caught in the back of his throat, making him cough. The ceiling was home to many cobwebs, with spiders breeding upon them.

Doug saw a shadow ahead and pointed his flashlight like a revolver. Ivy stood holding her teddy, ducking down from the floorboards above. She was shaking uncontrollably, the cold engulfing her and choking her breath. Her face was a mixture of shades of purple and blue.

"Baby, come here. Daddy is here," Doug called. She ran toward him, ramming herself into his arms. Doug, without another word, picked up his daughter and climbed out of the chilling darkness. "What happened, Princess?" Doug asked as he carried her through the downstairs hall.

"She told me to go to the basement. She locked me down there," she replied with a whisper.

Doug's blood felt even colder. "Who who locked you down there, angel?"

She looked into his eyes with a fearful, cold look. "Tabitha!"

8

A few days had passed since the cellar incident. Ivy had spent the last few nights sleeping in bed with Doug and Joanne and following Doug around like a lost puppy. It was a Friday night when Doug and Joanne wanted some alone time together, some quality time. Joanne had spoken to one of her work friends and asked if her daughter would babysit.

The babysitter was booked and a table reserved at a nice Italian restaurant. Doug stood in front of the bedroom wall mirror, gazing at his reflection. He was dressed in a clean, sharp-looking gray suit, with a slim-fitting blue shirt. Doug had risen to the occasion. He had showered and gotten his hair cut. He examined his look, checking himself out. *Not bad,* he thought in a modest tone.

Joanne came out of the en suite bathroom. Doug had been with Joanne for ten years, and had seen her at her best many times. However, she made his jaw drop tonight. She was wearing a gorgeous red gown. The dress had sheer, long sleeves embellished with tonal shimmering appliques.

The sweetheart neckline showed off the applique at the bodice. With a rich play on texture, the skirt had a subtle sweep, with a full-length hem. Her strawberry-blond hair curled from about midway, flowing down the front of her dress.

"You look stunning," Doug said, his tongue rolling out of his mouth.

Joanne, seeing Doug's reaction to her dress, smiled at him. "Not bad yourself," she replied. The two walked down the stairs, crisscrossing hands. The babysitter stood by the door, looking in awe at the couple walking down the stairs. "You look beautiful, Mrs. Moore," she said. Joanne smiled.

"I have left my number on the coffee table," Doug said. "Help yourself to anything you need." The parents kissed their two children and left the house. The trip to Denbigh was only a short twenty minutes. The town was lit up. Streetlights stood like soldiers in position across the town.

Doug had booked Con Amici, an Italian restaurant situated in the lower area of Denbigh. The exterior had a large tarmac lot to the front. The building was two stories high, with three slate roofs of mixed-size tiles.

The double-door front entrance was crafted from beechwood, with custom-made windows above it. The exterior of the building was lit with small, round absinthe lights with two main lights shining above the entrance, flooding it with a bright glow.

The main doors had two single panes of glass, each bearing the badge of the Prince of Wales with its three feathers. The main sign, resting above the doorway, bore a mixture of the colors of the Italian flag-red, green, and white and spelled the words *Con Amici.*

The House

Doug parked the car and walked to the passenger side, being a gentleman, and opened the door, giving Joanne a hand to help her out. They crossed the lot and walked through the entrance, with the lights beaming down on them from above, and were greeted by a teenage girl; Doug noticed her candy-colored nails and the neon shoelaces peeking out from under her pale-looking uniform.

"Good evening, welcome to Con Amici," she said happily. "Table for two, sir?"

Doug smiled at the welcoming girl. "Good evening. Yes, please," he replied. They followed her from the entrance and through the main bar area.

There were three coffee tables positioned at different points in the room surrounded by leather couches and small egg-shaped leather seats. The base of the bar was made with stonework similar to the exterior of the building, with an oak surface atop. There was a vast selection of beers, ciders, liquors, and wines. Doug felt uneasy as he passed.

The main seating area was well lit, with five candle lamps hanging over various sections of the room. The center of the room held many oak tables, each with four red-leather chairs, with the walls lined by moon-shaped booths with small, round tables. On the wall on the far side of the room hung a black-and-white picture of two men playing pool and having a discussion with each other.

The waitress pointed them toward one of the booths. "I think this table will be to your liking, sir," she said as she placed the cutlery down. As Doug and Joanne took their seats, some local men gaped in awe of Joanne's dress.

A single candle twinkled on the table. The waitress soon returned with menus, which had extensive choices for meals and appetizers, a few of which were from different countries such as England and France, but most of which were Italian.

"Can I get you anything to drink?" the waitress asked.

Doug looked to Joanne with rueful hope. She saw this and nodded in approval. "Just one," she added with a small smile. Doug smiled, excitement setting in. He kissed her in thanks.

"I'll have a pint of Foster's, and a glass of rose for my wife, please," Doug said quickly, the need for the alcohol yearning inside him. She returned five minutes later with the drinks, taking their order for food. At last they were alone, something that had not happened for some time. Doug grabbed her hand, stroking her fingers. He found this therapeutic.

"These past few weeks have been crazy," Doug began as he bit down on a breadstick.

Joanne nodded in agreement. "I know. Poor Ivy she has had a terrible time lately."

Doug continued to eat the breadstick. Joanne began staring into space, her eyes glazed.

"You ok, sweetheart?" Doug said, concerned. No response. "Joanne!" Doug said, raising his voice slightly.

She twitched back into normality. "Sorry-was just thinking about Ivy. Excuse me. Need to use the bathroom," she said with an angry expression on her face. She stood up and left for the bathroom.

9

Georgia Giordano had not done much babysitting. She had only taken this job for the money. The money would go toward her summer holiday in Magaluf. Her mother had asked her that afternoon if she would do it, and at first she refused. However, when told she would receive forty pounds, she jumped at the chance. Forty pounds for a night was a good wage for a couple of hours of work.

The eighteen-year-old girl was not very tall, about five foot five, with breast-length curly black hair. Her skin was olive toned; that was from her Italian heritage. Having tucked the girls into bed, she sat on the couch in the study, watching a romantic comedy on television, with a bowl of popcorn and a cup of tea she was all set.

The house was cold this evening. A chill seemed to surround the house, even though the fire was still burning, the logs crackling as they were tickled by the warm flames. Georgia pulled a large woolen throw over herself, trying to conserve heat. She felt an eerie wisp of wind, then saw a shadow looming from the depths behind her.

She turned to look, but saw nothing. "Get a grip, Georgia," she scoffed. She turned back to face the television.

The wisp slowly passed her again. This time, Georgia swore she heard a woman laughing.

"Who's there?" she called, getting to her feet. The breeze responded with a gust that extinguished the flames in the fireplace. The television shut off without warning, leaving the room in complete darkness. Georgia now felt her heart thumping in her chest. Sweat formed on her forehead. *There is someone here,* she thought.

Suddenly a loud creak came from the stairs, then the sound of footsteps ascending them. To Georgia's horror, she heard the chilling sound of nails scraping along the walls. The temperature of the air around her was falling below zero. The world around her melted away. Her sole attention was on the slow scraping sound, like nails on a chalkboard.

The footsteps got to the top of the staircase, and the scraping suddenly stopped. The house was silent. The only sound came from Georgia's breathing.

The silence was broken by a noise that filled her heart with dread the creaking sound of a doorknob slowly being turned. Whispering a few words of encouragement to herself, Georgia ascended the stairs toward the landing. She could still hear the doorknob being slowly turned. As she reached the top, she noticed that the door to the girls' room was open.

Her heart sank. The door was wide open, and not a sound came from the room. She crept toward it, her mind racing and fear running to all points of her body. Goosebumps rose like little mountains on her skin. She reached the door, peering into the darkness; she could not see anything in front of her.

The House

She flipped the switch, flooding the room with light. The two girls were sleeping in bed, both cuddling their teddy bears. She shook her head in relief. *I must have been hearing things spooky.* She turned the light off and started to descend the staircase. A sudden forceful push from behind sent Georgia cascading down the stairs like a slinky, hitting her head on each step as she went down. The world in front of her was spinning, and with one final thump, it went black.

10

Doug and Joanne pulled up outside the house. At the restaurant, Joanne had left the table for a full thirty minutes, claiming she had a bad stomach. After this they had a good evening. Doug ordered a margherita pizza made with fresh tomatoes and mozzarella, with a hint of basil. Joanne ordered spaghetti ai frutti di mare, a spaghetti dish made with king prawns, baby prawns fresh squid, mussels, chilies, fresh ground garlic, red onion, tomato and cream. Joanne had told Doug that it was scrumptious. He took her word for it.

The night had been enjoyable, a relaxing evening after the weeks they had been through. The two had reminisced about their lives before having children. They had even relived the moment they had met.

The night they met was a cold one in the middle of November. Doug had been invited to join his friends for a night out with the guys. The guys, however, had joined up with a group of five girls, one of them being Joanne. Doug remembered the moment he first set eyes on her.

Joanne was standing by the bar with her friends. She was wearing a lace-back, cutout body-con dress. It was cream in

The House

color. Her hair was a bit shorter then. Her eyes were blue. Not just any blue-blue like a crystal-clear blue sea shimmering in the lights. She looked into his eyes, sucking him in; he could hear the seaside in his mind, the waves crashing against the shore. The group of guys walked over, and Doug made sure he introduced himself to Joanne first.

Doug remembered the first time he took hold of her hand as he introduced himself. "My name is Doug." Her smile made his knees buckle. He was instantly in love with this girl; she had him under her spell.

Doug didn't remember much more after that he got blind drunk. He learned the details at later points in his life, such as at his wedding. His best man, James, told the room about how that night Doug had told the group he was a millionaire. Joanne, knowing he was lying, somehow fell in love with Doug, mostly his boyish charm.

Doug smiled to himself while pulling the keys out of the ignition. *Those were the days,* he thought. They left the car, with Doug again opening the door for Joanne, and walked up the stairs. The house was in darkness. Opening the door, they heard sound of the television coming from the study.

Georgia was asleep on the couch. Doug walked toward the couch, throwing his coat onto an armchair. "Georgia," he said, hoping not to startle her. No response. He shook her shoulder.

"Georgia," he said loudly. Still no response.

"Doug!" Joanne shouted from upstairs.

Doug looked up toward the stairs. Her voice sounded distressed. "What?" he shouted.

"Ivy is missing!"

At first he thought he misheard his wife. He rushed up the stairs toward the room. The door was wide open. It was true. Ivy was not in her bed; her bed was empty. The parents looked at each other in alarm. Ivy was missing!

11

His child was missing; Ivy was missing. He thrashed through the house in search of her. He looked in every room on the top floor, under beds, in wardrobes. Joanne was sobbing in the hallway as he searched the rooms. Doug was screaming at the top of his lungs, "Ivy, Ivy." Doug moved downstairs to search the lower floor. He searched the kitchen, dining room, cellar, and finally returned to the study.

Once the panic set in, it was all he could focus on. He walked over to Georgia once more, holding a glass of water. "Georgia!" he shouted. She gave no response. Doug threw the water over her. She gasped for air, sitting upright. A large bump was forming on her forehead.

"What the hell are you doing sleeping?" Doug boomed with a tone of pure anger.

"I wasn't sleeping, Mr. Moore. I was pushed down the stairs," Georgia replied, holding her head, which was pounding in pain.

"So let me get this straight someone pushed you down the stairs and then put you on the couch?" Doug said, anger raging through his veins.

"Mr. Moore, I swear I was pushed. Look at the bump on my head," she said, cowering as Doug rose over her.

"Ivy is missing," Joanne shouted at Georgia.

Georgia's face filled with horror, sheer panic taking over. "Missing? She was in bed when I checked on them. That's when I heard the footsteps going up the stairs."

Doug laughed sarcastically. "You're a liar," he yelled at her. "I'm calling the police!"

12

Communications operator Mason had worked for Denbighshire Police for eight years. She had worked within the main control center for her whole time of service. The control center was based within Denbighshire Business Park. The room itself was massive and square in shape. You could have fit four football fields within it. Five large air-conditioning pillars stood in a row in the middle of the room.

Banks of desks ran the length of the room. On the far left-hand side of the room was a high, raised platform with a single desk. This was the area of the control room inspector. He or she controlled all the activities for the incidents being handled in the room. These inspectors were called FIMs, which stood for force incident manager.

The role Mason had played within the center had changed many times. She was first a call handler, taking incoming non-emergency and emergency calls and creating incident reports thereafter. She then progressed on to a dispatcher, in which she dispatched incoming incidents to officers on the ground. However, to save money, the geniuses upstairs decided to merge the two roles together, calling the new role a communications operator.

The evening was already dragging. She had started at seven o'clock and was looking forward to the end of the shift at four in the morning. Not many calls had come in since she had started. It was nearly a quarter to eleven-only fifteen minutes before her lunch break. Suddenly a loud bleep sounded in her ear. She looked at the screen of her ICCS electronic computer telephone. In the bottom corner of the screen, a small red box flashed as the emergency call was placed through from the BT exchange.

"Police emergency," Mason greeted the caller.

"Hello, hello, I need the police! My daughter is missing. I cannot find her," a male voice shouted in a panic-stricken tone.

"Sir, calm down. What is your name?" Mason replied calmly.

"Doug, Doug Moore," he said. "I live in the house just by Llyn Alwen."

"Right, got it. And your daughter, how old is she?" Mason asked, beginning to complete an incident log.

"She is four years old. Her name is Ivy."

"Ok, and when was she last seen?"

"The babysitter says she last saw her about a quarter to ten."

"Ok, and have you searched the whole house, including the yard?"

"Yes, of course I have," Mr. Moore snapped at her.

The House

She ignored the anger in Doug's tone of voice. "Ok, Mr. Moore, what is she wearing, and what does she look like?"

"She is short, with shoulder-length brown hair. She's wearing her *Frozen* pajama top and bottoms."

"Ok, now, does she know her way around?" Mason asked, placing the incident on the pending screen for the dispatchers to get officers to the scene.

"Not really she just knows the house and the yard, and she is in neither," he stammered.

"Ok, Mr. Moore, we will have police officers with you shortly. Hang tight."

"Ok, thank you," he said. The line went dead.

Poor family must be worried sick, she thought.

The FIM stood up, shouting at the dispatchers who covered the area of the incident. "I want all available resources at that location, and I want them there now," he ordered. "I also want a bronze commander at the scene. Ask the local sergeant to take the role of bronze and to make it to the scene immediately."

The dispatcher nodded. "Yes, sir."

13

Sergeant Anthony Lomax was the night sergeant covering the whole of the rural area of Conwy Borough. He sat at his desk checking the incoming events on his screen. A red flashing event came through showing a high-risk missing person. He clicked on the event. Horror struck him when he saw the address. He knew this place.

A strong male voice crackled on his personal radio. "TA to Sierra 315."

Lomax picked up his radio. "Go ahead," he replied, speaking into the microphone on the radio.

"Sgt, we have a high-risk missing person. A four-year-old child."

"I have just seen the event; I want all units from all the areas to make it to the scene."

"Copy that, Sgt," the voice replied. "The FIM is asking you to take the role of bronze."

"Roger, will do. I'll head to the scene now." Lomax stood, pulling on his Kevlar stab-resistant vest. He then pulled on his load vest, which held his handcuffs, baton, and CS spray. Grabbing the car keys for his Ford Focus response vehicle, he left the station.

The House

The Focus roared to life. Placing the car into gear, he left the lot. He turned on the blue strobe emergency lights, which danced in the night sky. He left the sirens off, as it was late. He sped along the country lanes. The Focus performed in the weather conditions, sticking to the tarmac, the tires biting in deep, the rubber burning under the pressure.

Lomax knew this road well. He kept his eyes sharp on the road ahead. On many bends, he was driving on the wrong side of the road. He kept his wits about him. Many local boys were known to race on these roads in the dead of night.

The blue strobe lights flooded the road. Ahead of him were two more sets of blue lights. Local officers must have beaten him to the scene. Lomax turned off the lights, pulling into the driveway of the house. Lomax got out of the vehicle and walked up to closest PC.

"Sergeant," the PC said with a nod, as he wrote something in his pocket notebook.

"What's the situation? Have we found the child yet?" Lomax asked, placing his peaked cap in position.

"No, Sgt. We checked the surrounding areas. However, we've found nothing."

"Ok, I'll request NPAS from the control room and make contact with mountain rescue," Lomax replied.

NPAS, which stood for National Police Air Service, had twenty air bases located across the United Kingdom. It was a national service that was regionally coordinated for local delivery.

"TA from 315," Lomax said into his radio.

"Go ahead, Sergeant," a new female voice said.

"I need NPAS assistance, and also I need a SARDA dog, so mountain rescue needs to be requested."

"Roger. We will contact them now," she replied. SARDA was the Search and Rescue Dog Association.

"NPAS, TA." A male voice with a strong Merseyside accent came over the air. The sound of the roaring engines of the helicopter nearly drowned out his voice.

"Go ahead, NPAS."

"Thank you. We have just lifted from base. Our ETA to scene is five minutes."

"Roger, thank you."

NPAS, based in Deeside, was not far from the scene. The helicopter could already be heard in the distance as it glided through the skies.

The aircraft was equipped with state-of-the-art technology. Situated under the nose of the aircraft was a SkyQuest digital image recorder, with daylight and thermal imaging lenses. A digital downlink was located on the stern of the aircraft. This device allowed encrypted images from the aircraft to be relayed and watched on monitors within the police control room.

Below the tail of the aircraft was a light called the Nitesun, which emitted the equivalent of thirty million candlepower bulbs. The final bit of equipment on board was the SkyForce mapping system, a GPS-based map display with an integrated navigation and task management system built in.

Lomax could see the light from the helicopter's tail lighting system in the dark canopy above. It was a clear sky tonight.

The House

The stars were scattered like a hand had thrown moon dust into the sky. The helicopter hovered above like a buzzard stalking its prey. "NPAS at scene," the pilot shouted into the radio.

"Roger."

"Do we have a bronze on the ground?" the pilot asked.

"Yes, yes, it's Sierra 315," the operator replied.

"NPAS to Sierra 315."

"Go ahead."

"Have we got a search perimeter?"

"If a ten-mile radius can be searched from your point above."

"Got that; will search now." The helicopter began its search.

Lomax approached the front door of the house, remembering that he had come here a few times before, and walked in. The parents of the child sat in the study on a leather couch. "Mr. and Mrs. Moore?"

Mr. Moore looked up at him, and then rose to his feet. "Yes," he replied.

"I am Sergeant Lomax from Denbigh Police Station," he said, taking Mr. Moore's hand and shaking it. "Now, when did you last see your daughter?"

"She was last seen around a quarter to ten," Mr. Moore replied. "The babysitter said she heard footsteps going up the stairs and entering the girls' room. She says she walked into the room, and both girls were in bed." Mrs. Moore sobbed into her hands, and Mr. Moore put his arms around her.

"I see. And you returned home at what time?" Lomax asked, writing key points in his pocket notebook.

"My wife and I returned home around eleven thirty," Mr. Moore said timidly.

"Right. And I believe she was wearing *Frozen* pajama bottoms and top?" Mr. Moore nodded at Lomax.

"Ok, do you mind if I check the room?" Lomax asked.

"Of course not," Mr. Moore replied.

"This officer will continue to take your statement." Lomax walked up the staircase, flashbacks playing in his head. He moved into the children's bedroom. The air within was full of fear and despair. Lomax searched around the room, checking the bed and under it. However, he found nothing.

As he pulled the bedside table away from the wall, a small teddy bear fell to the floor. Lomax's eyes widened with alarm. The bear's arm was missing; the bottom half of the bear was covered in blood. Lomax stared at the bear in horror. He pulled his radio from his load vest. "315, urgent!" he said, panic in his voice.

"Sergeant, go ahead."

"I need CID here, and I need them now."

14

Detective constable Gary Philips sat at his desk alone, gazing at his computer screen. It had just turned midnight. As always, it was a quiet weekday night. There were only three night-shift detective constables on duty, along with one detective sergeant.

Philips sat there twiddling his thumbs, bored out of his mind. His other two colleagues had their heads buried in their paperwork and case files. Philips, on the other hand, sat there smugly, shaking his head at them.

He had no paperwork to complete, no files to prepare. Philips was known for his impeccable handling of his workload. He was a very driven detective. He wanted nothing more than a promotion. Philips had not been a detective long, having passed the exams only eight months prior.

Philips had solved three armed robberies, seven burglaries, and one murder. The murder case was that of an old woman who had been killed by her grandson. Philips's superiors referred to him as Bolt due to the lightning speed with which he was able to investigate and apprehend a suspect. Philips only liked to take on the big cases. He felt his talents were worthy of dealing with major events, not low-level crime.

Detective sergeant Williams burst into the room, his tall, stocky presence towering over his detectives. "Right, gents," he said, clapping his hands together. "We've got a child abduction up at the house near Llyn Alwen."

Philips's colleagues looked up at one another in alarm. They then buried their heads in their work even further. "And, yes, I need a willing volunteer." The detectives' faces got lower and lower, nearly pressing against their papers.

Sergeant Williams turned to face Philips. Philips looked away; he hated abduction cases. "Philips, my office, now!" Williams roared. Philips huffed, pulling his athletically built body from its chair and pushing his light-blond hair to the side. His deep-hazel colored eyes glazed with boredom.

Philips walked to the sergeant's office, which was a large room just off the main CID room. Sergeant Williams sat with his feet up on the desk. "Ah, Philips, sit down please," Williams said, pointing at the chair in front of the desk.

Philips took a seat, crossing his legs.

"I know you don't like investigations like this one," he began.

"Sgt, please don't give me this case," Philips begged.

Williams raised a hand in protest. "This is not a debate, Philips. This is a serious abduction a four-year-old child was abducted from her room, with no suspects at this time. The only evidence left was a blood-soaked teddy bear belonging to the little girl."

When he heard the word *blood*, Philips's ears perked up. "Has a body been found?" Philips asked, intrigued.

The House

Sergeant Williams shook his head. "No," Williams replied. "The child has gone without a trace. I need my best detective on this, Philips. Also, if you solve this one, I can feel a detective sergeant promotion following it."

Those words rang in Philips's ears. A promotion that's what he wanted. He wanted to be a detective sergeant. Philips stood up and walked to the door of the sergeant's office. "I'll take the case. Leave it to me," Philips said as he walked out, moving to his desk.

He picked up his personal radio, his overcoat, and his car keys.

"Be careful with this one, Gary," one of his colleagues shouted at him.

"What do you mean?" he asked, buttoning up his overcoat.

The detective looked at him with a concern look on his face. "Just be careful."

15

Doug stood at the kitchen window, staring out into the dark forest in front of him. His world was moving in slow motion. Police officers walked around taking pictures. Strange men in white overalls with hoods, wearing rubber gloves and blue breathing masks, dusted for fingerprints.

The outside of his house was lit up like it was Christmastime. The flicker of red-and-blue lights danced with the shadows of the night. A muffled noise came from behind him, the sound of someone calling him from a far-away distance.

"Mr. Moore," a young officer said, patting him on the shoulder.

He jumped slightly, not expecting it. "Sorry. I was in a world of my own," Doug replied.

"It's ok, sir. Sergeant Lomax has asked if you will see him in the bedroom, please," the officer said sternly.

It sounded serious. Doug nodded politely and walked up to the children's bedroom. Lomax stood in front of him, holding an evidence bag that had been sealed and marked. Doug took hold of the bag, peering through the thin plastic.

The House

His hands turned into jelly, and all the feeling in his fingers drained away. The bag fell from his grip. His hands began to shake, and his face went white. Doug stumbled backward. "Ivy's t-t-eddy," he stammered, his eyes welling up with tears.

"This is Ivy's teddy, is it?" Lomax said in a compassionate tone as he picked up the bag. Doug was unable to speak; tears rolled down his cheeks as he stood in silence. "Mr. Moore, please sit down," Lomax said quietly as he guided Doug down. "I regret to have to tell you this, but I think we are looking at a child abduction here."

The words hit him like he had been shot. "But who who could have done this?" Doug said, wiping tears away from his eyes.

Before Lomax could answer, another officer came into the room. "Sgt, DC Philips has just passed the outer checkpoint. He will be here in a minute."

"Thank you," Lomax said. "Mr. Moore, perhaps you should follow me." Lomax walked to the door.

Doug got to his feet, his legs feeling like jelly. *How am I going to tell Joanne?* he thought. Doug followed Lomax down the stairs into the front garden. A fresh set of headlights could be seen pulling up, and soon a dark-blue Volkswagen Passat rumbled down the bumpy driveway.

It stopped in front of them, and a young man got out. He wasn't very tall, had an athletic build, and was wearing a dark-gray tailored suit with a pure-white shirt and a black tie. He walked over in an important manner. "Sergeant." He nodded toward Lomax.

"Gary, this is Mr. Moore. He is the father of the child."

Philips turned to Doug. "Mr. Moore, I am Detective Constable Philips. I am taking over the investigation of your daughter's disappearance," he said.

"Nice to meet you, Detective," Doug said, shaking his hand.

Philips turned back to face Lomax. "Has NPAS turned up anything?"

Lomax shook his head. "Nothing on the open areas. However, the wooded areas are too dense for their thermals."

"I heard SARDA had been requested?" Philips asked, looking around.

"They have been contacted; however, they wont be available until morning," Lomax replied. "And we don't currently have any police dog handlers on duty."

"Mr. Moore, can we speak inside?" Philips asked, moving toward the door. Doug followed, opening the front door for him.

Doug led him down into the kitchen, which was the least crowded area of the house, and pulled out a stool for Philips to sit on. "Can I get you a drink?" Doug asked.

"No, thank you," Philips replied, pulling out his notebook. "So Mr. Moore, have there been any strangers hanging around the house lately?"

Doug shook his head. "No, no one. I haven't seen a single person pass the house since we moved in."

Philips began to jot down the information in his notebook. "Has anything come to your attention? Has your daughter's character been out of sorts?" Philips asked.

The House

"Well, since moving here, she has had a child's illusion that a doll called Tabitha is after her. She said the doll was 'trying to make her dead," Doug said. "I didn't take her seriously until her school teacher told me she had broken down in class."

"Where is this doll now?" Philips said, looking up at Doug with interest at this information.

"I threw it away. I dumped it a long way from here," Doug replied, looking at his hands.

"Interesting," Philips said, writing further information in his book.

Joanne came from around the corner. "Who is this?" she asked, looking in Philips's direction.

"Sweetheart, this is Detective Constable Philips. He is taking charge of the investigation," Doug said, rushing to her side. Her cheeks flushed red as anger took hold of her.

"If he is in charge of looking for Ivy, then what is he doing sitting in our kitchen?" she shouted.

"Mrs. Moore, please calm down. I am just asking some questions that may help us find your daughter that's is all," Philips said as he stood up.

"What is it you want to know?" Joanne asked.

"Mrs. Moore, have you seen any strangers hanging around the house over the past couple of days?"

"No, no one walks around here. We haven't had any visitors," she replied.

"And where were you both at the time of the disappearance?"

"Why are you asking the same questions? We already answered that question," she spat. "We went out for a meal at Con Amici in Denbigh and we came home around eleven-thirty."

"Did anyone approach your table while you were at Con Amici?"

Doug looked at him, slightly confused. "What do you think that someone followed us to Con Amici and then came back and abducted our daughter?"

"It's not impossible. I'm just trying to cover all bases."

"Well I had a dodgy stomach, so I was in the bathroom for thirty minutes, so I don't know. Doug, did anyone come to the table?" Joanne asked.

"Well," Doug said nervously, "while you were in the bathroom, I went outside and had a couple more drinks."

"What do you mean you had a few more drinks?" Joanne said, now turning her displeasure toward Doug.

"We'll talk about this later," Doug said. He was looking at the detective, who seemed to want to move the conversation on.

"This is ridiculous. Find my daughter detective now!" She stormed out of the room.

The room was silent for a moment before Philips continued.

"Who was in charge of the girls while you went out?"

"We left them in the charge of a babysitter, a daughter of one of my wife's work friends."

Philips went silent while he wrote. Doug felt unease wash over him. Philips pocketed his notebook and looked at Doug

The House

for a brief moment, analyzing him. Doug, feeling even more unnerved, coughed aloud. "Detective, is there a problem?"

Philips shook his head. "No, Mr. Moore, I'm just thinking to myself-I do this a lot," Philips replied, trying to reassure Doug. Lomax entered the room, holding the plastic bag containing Ivy's teddy.

He passed it to Philips, who examined the teddy. "Where was this found?" he asked, looking at Lomax.

"It was found behind the bedside table. Perhaps the abductor hid it there so it wouldn't be found."

"Has any blood been found in the room?"

Lomax again shook his head. "No, we found nothing on the initial search. Crime scene investigators are searching the room now for more evidence."

Philips stood up and walked to the stairs. "Best take a look at the room." He disappeared up the stairs.

Doug looked at Lomax. "I better go and check on my wife." Doug stood up and walked into the dining room, where Joanne sat alone, staring out the window. She was holding one of Ivy's favorite teddies, caressing the soft woolen fur. Her eyes were red and raw from the buckets of tears she had shed. Doug walked over to her, throwing his arms around her waist.

She turned to look at her husband. "Where is our little girl? What has happened to her?" She sobbed, stroking the teddy even more.

"We will find her even if I have to look day and night. I promise you I will find her," Doug said loudly. The worried parents embraced further, and Doug kissed Joanne on the forehead. Philips cleared his throat from the staircase.

"Mr. Moore, can I speak with you briefly?"

Doug left Joanne's side and walked back into the hallway.

"I need to speak to your other daughter, Raine, if that's ok with you?" Philips asked.

"It that necessary?" Doug replied, looking back at Joanne.

"She may be able to offer us some more information, as she and Ivy shared a room."

"Ok, but she is very tired, so can we make it quick?"

"Of course," Philips said.

The two walked back up the staircase and walked into the main bedroom, where Raine sat alone on the bed.

"Sweetheart," Doug said, walking toward her. "Mr. Philips here is a police man, and he has some questions he would like to ask you. Is that ok?"

Raine looked up at him with tears forming in the corner of her eyes. She nodded.

Philips now took Doug's place, sitting beside Raine.

"Hello Raine, my name is Gary, and I'm here to try and find Ivy, but I'm going to need your help, ok?" Philips said, smiling kindly.

"Ok," Raine replied. The tears dropped from her eyes to the ground.

"Did you hear anything after Georgia the babysitter put you to bed?"

Raine shook her head. "No, I was asleep. I did have a scary dream, though," she said, more tears building.

The House

"What nightmare was this?" Philips said, looking intrigued.

"I had a dream where I could not see anything-the room was black-but I heard this sound, this scary sound." Raine replied, beginning to shake with fear.

"Detective, I think that's enough for one night," Doug said, placing his hand on Raine's shoulders.

"Mr. Moore, please," Philips said, disgruntled at the interruption. He turned a smile back to Raine. "What was this sound you heard?"

"It, it was a scraping sound, like something scraping along a wall, but I couldn't see anything. But the sound-it was scary."

"So you didn't hear any screaming, nothing at all?" Philips said.

"No, I did not hear anything else," she said, breaking into tears. Doug pulled her into a tight hug.

"Ok, I think that is enough now," Philips said, patting Raine on the back.

"Did I help?" Raine said, turning to face Philips, her cheeks soaked.

"You did great, Raine, you helped in a big way," Philips said with one last big smile.

"Sweetheart why don't you get into Mummy and Daddy's bed; I'll be back up soon, ok?" Doug said, kissing her on the forehead. Raine climbed under the covers.

Doug and Philips walked back down the stairs into the main hallway.

"I am going to leave two constables here with you overnight. The specialist search dogs aren't available until the early morning. I've got local patrols out looking on the roads in nearby villages, and few brave officers have taken some torches into the woods. I've got an officer taking a statement from the babysitter back at her house. I've got the control room checking the hospitals, and I will keep you updated," Philips said, checking his watch. "I will return in the morning when the search dogs arrive." He held his hand out. "Goodnight, Mr. Moore. Try to get some sleep."

"Good night, Detective. We will try." Doug shook his hand. He left, leaving Doug and Joanne alone in the study.

16

The morning sun rose over the mountains, casting a dull light across the valley. The air was chilling, with a sense of despair stewing within it. The wind did not blow this morning; the valley was silent. Not even the birds sang.

Doug hadn't slept a wink. He had tossed fitfully all night, playing over the possibilities of what might have happened to his child. Joanne had taken some calming pills, which made her drowsy, and she had fallen asleep.

Doug got out of bed and walked downstairs to the kitchen. He peered out the window at the front porch. The two police officers still stood outside; they must have been freezing. Doug walked to the door, opening it to speak to them.

"Officers, do you fancy a cup of tea? You must be freezing out here," Doug said in a concerned tone. The officers smiled and nodded at his offer. He made them two cups of tea, and placed assorted biscuits on a plate.

"How did you sleep, Mr. Moore?" the small, chubby officer asked him.

"I didn't sleep well at all," he said, shaking his head. "All I could think about was my daughter."

"We'll find her, sir, you wait and see," the officer said, patting him on the shoulder encouragingly.

The morning dragged by. Doug's mind was still only on one thing. Earlier, he had informed Ivy's school about the incident. The headmistress expressed her sympathies, offering the full support of the school.

At 9:00 a.m., he heard tires rumbling down the gravel track toward the house. He walked to the windows to see DC Philips, as promised, returning to the house. He was on the phone, talking hurriedly.

As he opened the front door, Doug heard parts of Philips's conversation.

"No, sir, nothing has turned up yet." Pause. "No, sir, no ransom demand has been made yet. I will be requesting a search team and will speak with POLSA."

By POLSA he meant Police Search Advisor, a person who acted as a manager of a highly trained team of search officers. They were utilized for searching for evidence of crimes and missing persons.

"Also, I will liaise with the FIM regarding an underwater team to search the lake."

Doug felt his heart drop. What if she had been drowned and left to sink to the dark depths of the lake?

DC Philips coughed, bringing Doug out of his concerned daydream. "Mr. Moore, good morning."

"Good morning, Detective. Please call me Doug," Doug said.

The House

Philips moved into the kitchen, pulling out his notebook. "Doug, I forgot to ask last night. Have any strange incidents occurred in or around the house recently?"

Doug looked down at the floor. *Should I tell him? He won't believe me even if I do.*

"No, it's a normal house," Doug lied. "Well, now that you mention it, there was a woman who stopped me while I was walking around the lake. It was about two weeks ago. She warned me."

"Warned you about what?" Philips asked.

"Well, she told me that I should get out now. She said she 'will come for you and kill you all.' No idea who she was referring to."

Philips wrote frantically in his notebook. "Do you know her name?" Philips asked. His excitement at this new information was clear.

Doug scanned his memories of that day as if he could forget that evil cackle and her figure pointing at him from the distance. "Belinda Black. She is an old woman. I'm not sure where she lives," Doug said.

"Belinda Black," Philips repeated, writing the name down. "Bear with me." Philips pulled out his personal radio. "TA from Delta 2566," he said into the radio microphone.

"Delta 2566, go ahead," replied a polite female voice.

"Can I have a person checked? Location Denbigh Moors."

"Go ahead with your details. Over."

"Belinda Black, no date of birth," Philips said, shutting his notebook.

"Roger, standby."

There was a short silence while the operator completed the search. "TA, Delta 2566."

"Go ahead, TA."

"Thank you. Belinda Black has no forwarding address. However, a search shows that she is known to live within a shack in the woods near Llyn Alwen."

"Roger, thank you." Philips stood, pulling his mobile out of his pocket. He spoke on the phone for ten minutes, leaving Doug sitting in the kitchen.

"TA, Delta 2566,"

"Go ahead," Philips said.

"To advise you, POLSA and his search team are en route to scene now."

"Roger, thank you." Philips walked back in the room.

"Doug, do you think you could show me where you came across this lady?" he asked.

Doug stood up. A feeling of purpose overcame him. He could help in the search of his daughter. "Yes, certainly." Doug walked to the study, picked up his jacket, and headed for the door.

17

Doug and Philips marched out of the house and headed for the path that led to the lake. Doug retraced his steps to the forest where he had met Belinda Black. The morning sun shone down on them, the sunlight bursting through the thick canopy above.

The forest was a lot lighter this time around, and the air was more open, with no fear lingering within it. They continued on to the point where Doug had come across Belinda Black. There was no sign of her. "This is where I met her. She came walking out of nowhere toward me," Doug said, pointing in the direction she came from.

They continued to search the woods for the shack. A hundred feet in front of them, a small, oval-shaped clearing came suddenly into view. Within the clearing stood a two-story wooden shack.

It was built from wood made from the local conifer trees. A small porch led up to the wooden door. The door was covered in dead moss, and poison ivy drowned it. The house only had two windows, which were located on the top floor of the shack and were oval in shape with old-style curtains drawn across them, with only a small opening between the curtains. The house had a creepy aura about it. Doug looked more closely at the house. He was sure it was leaning to one side. Doug and Philips moved closer to the house.

"This must be the house," Philips said, convinced. "Looks like the sort of place she would live in."

Doug agreed. The two moved in closer. Doug's heart began to beat faster and faster as they approached the front door.

Philips went first, walking up the steps to the porch. Near the door, an old rocking chair eerily creaked back and forth. No one sat in it. Doug's skin began to crawl, his spine tingling. Philips moved to the door, extended his hand, and knocked on the door.

The door slowly creaked open. It was not shut in the first place. Philips looked at Doug and then slowly walked into the house. Doug followed behind him. The house had an open plan, with no walls separating the rooms.

Six wooden pillars supported the upper floor of the house. The pillars were rotting slowly away as woodworms devoured them from within. A narrow bamboo staircase led to a lone room on the upper floor, which had a dirty single mattress for a bed.

The kitchen area had an old-style cooker with one hob. A small dining table, caked in dust, appeared not to have been eaten on for some time. Rotten food littered the table, flies feasting on the festering food.

The sink was weighed down with plates and pots, also covered in food and dust. One main light hung from the

The House

center point of the roof. Parts of the house were in darkness, as the light was not strong enough to cover the whole bottom floor.

Both jumped and turned toward the kitchen when they heard a sudden noise, followed by a flurry of movement. Doug swung to the left in fright, his arms shaking. A fat black cat sat on the table, staring coldly at the two strangers in his house. His piercing yellow eyes scanned their every movement.

"Shoooo," Philips shouted at the cat, trying to frighten it off. The cat stared on further, not blinking, not even twitching in fear. Doug backed away from the table slightly.

Chills raced up and down his spine, and his blood went cold in fear. From the darkness behind him, an old, wrinkly hand grabbed his shoulder, pressing down hard, digging into his flesh. He let out a scream of pain, running forward toward Philips.

"What the hell," Philips shouted.

From the shadows emerged the owner of the hand. A frail old woman stood before them. "Who dares enter my house uninvited?" she growled under her breath. Doug stood behind Philips, and the woman advanced toward them.

"Miss Black?" he asked in a tone of authority. She nodded sheepishly at him. "Miss Black, my name is Detective Constable Philips from Saint Asaph police station," he said, holding up his warrant card.

"And what would you be doing in my house, Detective?" Miss Black said, raising her walking stick into a defensive position.

"I am here investigating the disappearance of a young child," Philips replied.

Belinda looked at Philips for a moment. She began to laugh uncontrollably at Philips, holding her stomach as she did. "She struck again. I warned you, Dougy-Doug," she said, pointing her crooked finger at Doug. "And now she has your rat of a child."

Doug no longer felt fear, and he pushed forward. "What do you mean, 'rat'? Who are you calling a rat?" he said. Philips blocked him from advancing further.

Belinda moved to the table, continuing to laugh as she went. She sat at the table, stroking the fat, black cat, who began to purr. "All children are rats in my eyes. I warned you. I told you to leave the house, but you didn't listen, did you? Now look where that has gotten you," Belinda said. "You just ignored me, and now look one child missing."

"Miss Black, where were you last night around ten thirty?" Philips asked, changing the subject.

"Ha, looks like I'm a suspect," she chuckled. "I was here with Mr. Tudor, here alone all evening." She stroked the purring cat, which kept its watchful eyes on Philips and Doug.

"Anyone other than Mr. Tudor who can verify that?"

"Detective, I did not kidnap that little rat."

"Well, who did, Miss Black?" Philips asked in an impatient tone.

"She has her now. I'm surprised you don't know about the house, Detective, and the unsolved cases there."

"Unsolved cases? What do you mean, 'unsolved'?" Doug shouted from behind Philips.

The House

"Well, there have been past incidents at the house. That house has had more owners in the past five years than ever before," Belinda continued. "Other children have also disappeared from that house."

Doug looked away, thinking about the past couple of weeks the cellar incident, the eyeless woman on the road, Ivy's strange behavior.

"You know of what I speak," she said, pointing at Doug.

Philips continued to look at Belinda. "Miss Black, that's enough. Who is this woman you speak of?" Philips pressed on.

Belinda turned her head, her old bones cracking as her spine readjusted. An evil smirk slowly crept onto her face. "She is a terrible woman, with a wrath that would match the devil's. Her name is Nanny Moon!"

18

Philips looked at Belinda Black in confusion. "Nanny Moon," he said slowly. "And where does she live? What's her address?"

Black laughed again, throwing her head back. "You don't find Nanny Moon. She finds you."

"Who is she?" Doug asked.

She turned to look at Doug. "Her birth name was Nannette Moon. However, she was nicknamed Nanny Moon later in life. She was born in a small house somewhere in Clocaenog Forest."

"Clocaenog Forest?" Doug said.

"Yes it's about five minutes' drive from here," Belinda said, continuing to stroke her cat.

"Later in life, she became a nanny, looking after children of rich families. In 1878 she was employed by the richest family in the area, the Hughes family, who lived in your very house." Black coughed loudly into a soiled rag. "Mr. Hughes was the owner of a mining firm, so he was well off. They had two little rats themselves, Lilly and Thomas Hughes," she said with a look of disgust on her face.

The House

"Miss Black, where are you going with this?" Philips asked.

"You asked me a question, and I am telling you the answer," Black hissed. "She worked for the family for six years, becoming close to the children. She loved those children more than anything. However, in the autumn of 1884, both children went missing, gone without a trace." She coughed again and then continued. "Searches went on for days. They searched the woods, the lake, and the surrounding fields, and they found nothing."

"What happened to the children?" Doug asked.

"Well, the first child, the young boy, Thomas, was found strangled with a piece of rope by the shoreline of the lake," Belinda said, a small grin forming. "Forty-eight hours later, the little girl was found tied to tree, a short distance from the house. Her throat had been cut." She began to laugh aloud.

"You're evil. That's someone's child," Doug said to her as she banged her fist on the table in laughter.

"Like I said, rats. Rats' purpose in life is to be hunted and killed," Belinda replied, her grin shrinking away and anger now upon her face.

Philips took a seat at the table, notebook in hand. "Miss Black, continue. Who killed the little girls?" he asked, trying to bring her state of anger back to calm. Belinda, however, stared at Doug for a long five seconds before she spoke again.

"At the time, the police began an investigation," Belinda continued. "They discovered blood on Nanny's apron, and the blood-soaked knife that had been used to kill Lilly Hughes. Nanny Moon was instantly arrested by the local officers for the hideous murders she had committed."

"She was taken without a trial to the Hughes family, who brutally killed her," she said her serpent eyes glinting with malice.

Doug listened in horror, the blood draining from his face. "How was she murdered?" he asked.

A sardonic smile arched on her face. "Well, I'll tell you what they did," she said, sitting up in her chair. "They held her down. Mr. Hughes took out a large hunting knife, a needle, and thread." Her smile was getting wider. "He sewed her mouth closed while she was awake, drowning out her cries of pain. He then took the knife and cut out her eyes one by one, while she was still alive."

Doug held his hand over his mouth, a wave of nausea flowing up from his stomach.

"What did they do with the body?" Philips asked.

"They took her to the top of Craig Bron Bannog, dumped her body, and left her there to die."

Doug looked at Philips, in awe of the tale they had just been told. *Her eyes were cut out and her mouth was sewn shut-it couldn't be a coincidence,* Doug thought to himself.

"Miss Black, you're not seriously suggesting that a woman who was killed over a century ago has come from the dead to abduct a small girl?"

Black turned to look at Philips, distaste clear on her face. "You calling me a liar, Detective?" she asked with a growling tone.

The House

Philips casually stood up, huffing in annoyance. "You're wasting our time now, Miss Black, and, to be honest, I have better things to do than entertain your crazy stories."

Philips moved to the door, beckoning Doug to follow him. Doug, with his mind still racing, moved slowly toward the door. Unlike the detective, he had more questions than answers, with one question in particular screaming out at him.

"One second, Detective," Doug said, turning to face Black. "Who is Tabitha?"

Black looked at Doug for a moment; amazement was in her eyes. Philips looked at Black, awaiting her response, then looked at his watch.

Black coughed violently again, spitting into the soiled rag. "Tabitha is a doll that was said to have been given to the Hughes children by Nanny Moon as a present for Christmas one year," Black replied, pulling the rag from her mouth. "Some say that after her death, her spirit sought refuge within the doll to await her revenge on the world. However, to this day, it has never been seen again." Black looked at Doug in an inquisitive manner. "Why do you ask?"

"No reason," Doug lied. "Good-bye, Miss Black."

Doug turned on his heel, and they rushed out of the shack. Miss Black was not finished, however, and rose to her feet, pursuing them. "It's not too late, Doug! Leave the house now with the family you still have left," she barked, banging her walking stick on the wall.

"Stay away from my family, Miss Black," Doug warned. The two men continued away from the house, where Belinda stood watching from her porch.

"What did you think about her crackpot story? A load of rubbish, if you ask me," Philips said, looking at Doug, whose face was still icy white.

"I don't know," Doug lied.

"Really? Are you sure? You don't believe her, do you?" Philips said. "She's crazy."

"I just don't know. She knew about the doll, Tabitha," Doug said, thinking back to what she had just said. "Ivy kept using the name Tabitha, saying this doll was the reason she was feeling upset and that this doll had threatened to 'make her dead.'"

Philips stopped dead in his tracks, looking at Doug. "You never told me about the doll. Where was it found?"

"What do you mean?" Doug asked, confusion clear on his face.

"Simple question, Doug. Where was the doll found? Where did Ivy find it?"

Doug started searching his memory, thinking back to the first time he saw the doll. "Well, I found the doll on Raine's bed, but I don't know how it got there. There was lots of stuff left in the house when we moved in."

Philips continued to look at Doug. "Where is the doll now?" he asked.

"Well, when I realized that the doll was causing problems for Ivy, I drove it down to Llyn Brenig and threw it away."

Philips paused for a second. "I think we should speak to Raine and see if she remembers where the doll was found."

The two men shortly emerged out of the woodland. The officers still stood guard at the front of the house. "John,

The House

Phil, you can stand down and resume normal patrol," Philips ordered. The officers, with looks of unease on their faces, jumped at the chance to run back to their patrol vehicles.

Doug opened the door and was greeted by his wife. Joanne was still wearing her bedclothes, and Doug noticed bits of earth on her feet. "Sweetheart, where have you been?" Doug asked. She did not respond. Her face was haunted with grief. "Joanne," Doug said, grabbing her shoulder and looking into her cold eyes. "Joanne, where have you been?"

"I've been looking for Ivy," she whispered, tears rolling down her cheeks. She turned away and slowly walked up the stairs, dragging her feet as she went.

"Is she ok?" Philips asked, concerned.

"I'm not sure. She has been very quiet since the abduction."

"She is a distraught mother; it's understandable," Philips replied.

Doug walked up the stairs toward the girls' room. Raine sat on her bed, playing with her teddies.

"Princess," Doug said. She turned to look at him. "Can I speak to you for a second please?"

Raine smiled sweetly. "Yes, Daddy, what is it?"

"Do you remember that doll, Tabitha?" Doug asked. She nodded in reply. "Do you remember where you found it?"

"I found it on my bed when we came here," Raine replied.

"So who left it there?" Doug said, looking at Philips, who looked as confused as Doug did.

"I don't know, Daddy," she replied in an innocent tone.

Doug looked into his young daughter's beautiful hazel eyes. "Ok, Princess, thank you." Doug stood up and bent down, kissing Raine on the forehead.

"So who do you think left it on Raine's bed?" Philips asked.

Doug shook his head. "No idea. Must have been left here by the previous owners," Doug said as they left the bedroom. "I've been thing about what Miss Black said about the previous disappearances," Doug said.

Philips nodded in agreement. "I think I'll speak with Sergeant Lomax," Philips said, pulling on his overcoat.

"Can I come with you?" Doug asked eagerly, feeling the need to help further. He did not want to wait endlessly at home.

"Not sure if that is appropriate," Philips said, thinking.

"Please, Detective, let me help."

Philips thought for a short while. *If I was in this man's position and one of my children was missing, I would want to help too,* he thought to himself. Philips smiled at Doug. "Of course you can come, but if we are going to be partners, you really need to start calling me Gary."

Doug smiled. "You got it, Gary." Doug pulled on his coat from the rack.

The two men left the house, got into Philips's vehicle, and drove away, leaving Doug's family and the house behind.

19

Philips and Doug arrived at Denbigh Police Station. The main lot was guarded by a fob security iron gate. Philips pulled out a key from his breast pocket. The small gate-opening motor purred to life, and the gate slowly started opening.

Philips parked the car in one of the bays. As he got out of the vehicle, a strong autumn wind tumbled through the air, hitting him in the face, slapping his cheeks with cold. Doug followed him to the entrance of the station.

The station wasn't very large. In the main room, officers sat by their outdated computers, completing their mountains of paperwork from the day's incidents. An old printer on the far end of the room stood on a worn table.

Philips walked Doug through the room. Officers looked up at Doug with a hint of pity in their eyes, which made him feel uneasy. They stopped at the open door of a small box of a room. Sergeant Lomax sat at his desk talking on his phone. He saw the two men and waved them into his office.

He pointed to the seats in front of his desk. Doug and Philips sat down and waited a short period for Lomax to finish his telephone call.

"Evening, gentleman," he said, placing the receiver down.

"Sgt, anything from the SARDA team or POLSA?"

"Nothing." Lomax shook his head. "An extensive search of the woods has been done, and nothing."

"I have questioned a Miss Belinda Black today," Philips said, pulling out his notebook.

"Ah, you've spoken to old Belinda, have you?" Lomax replied, chuckling.

"She mentioned previous unsolved crimes and incidents taking place in Mr. Moore's house," Philips said to Lomax. "You wouldn't know anything about that, would you?"

Lomax glared at Philips, his face flushing in anger. "If I'm not mistaken, Detective, last time I checked, I still hold the rank of sergeant, and when you address me, you address me with a little more respect than that," Lomax boomed.

Philips, a little taken aback, looked at the floor for a moment. "I apologize," he said. "Could you tell us of any previous incidents at that house?"

Lomax paused for a moment, looking at Doug and then Philips. He stood from his chair, walked to the door of his office, and closed the door.

Lomax returned to his seat. "What has the old hag told you so far?" Lomax asked.

"Not much, just that there has been a previous disappearance from that house, and some murders in the past."

"Well, the first time the house came to my attention was about a year ago," Lomax began. "It was a similar night as to the last. A report came in that a child had been abducted

The House

from the address by unknown offenders. I was the first officer on scene. The family had been present at the time of the abduction. The father reported that he was sitting watching television when he heard footsteps slowly walking up to the second floor and a scratching noise against the walls. He then said he heard his son, Oliver, scream from the room. When he arrived in his son's room, Oliver had disappeared gone without a trace."

"Was a body ever found?" Philips asked, frantically writing Lomax's information down.

"No, they never found the body. However, for days the father insisted he heard someone or something walking up the stairs," Lomax said.

"What happened to the family?" Doug asked.

Lomax looked out the window for a second. Raindrops had begun beating upon on the glass. "They moved a month later, without a word, in the middle of the night."

"How old was the boy?" Philips asked.

"He was about the same age as Ivy. A bit older."

Doug's heart did a flip. What if they never found Ivy? How would he be able to live without knowing what happened to his daughter?

"What else happened in that house?" Philips asked, pushing the conversation on.

"Well, I looked into the house's history during the investigation of the boy's abduction," Lomax said, pulling a thick, blue file from a stack on his desk and thumbing through it. "Reports were made of strange break-ins in which the house was ransacked, strange items had been stolen, et cetera. I don't think a family has lived longer than seven months in that house," Lomax said, shutting the file. "They left without any good-byes or explanations, leaving their furniture and possessions behind, even the pictures on the walls."

"How many families have lived in the house over the past five years?" Philips asked.

Lomax counted in his head for a moment. "Including the Moores, that would be fifteen families," he replied.

"Fifteen," Doug repeated, astounded by the number.

"Yes, fifteen families. All moved with warning," Lomax said.

"You mentioned strange break-ins. What made them strange?" Philips inquired.

"Well, one family, about two years ago, moved in with their four children," Lomax began. "And one morning they came down to find the whole house turned over, and some family pictures had gone missing. They were never found."

Lomax's phone suddenly rang. "Sergeant Lomax," he answered. The distant voice of a girl could be heard. "One moment," he said, holding his hand over the receiver. "This is a victim call, if you have no further questions."

Philips smiled and closed his book. "Thanks, Sergeant."

Doug and Philips stood up, nodded to Lomax, and left his office. The conversation had left Doug feeling uneasy. Lomax had had some answers, but they just led to more and more questions in Doug's mind.

"You ok, Doug?" Philips asked, noticing the distress on Doug's face.

The House

"I'm just worried about Ivy, that's all," he said, holding back the urge to cry.

"Listen, we will find this son of a bitch and get your daughter back. You mark my words," Philips said, patting Doug on the back. Doug nodded sheepishly in agreement as they headed to the car.

However, as they drove home, Doug's mind replayed all the strange things that had happened in the house. One main question kept screaming at him: *Where was Ivy, or what had happened to her?*

20

Doug awoke. He was face down in dust. He pulled himself upward. He was in a long rectangular room. The walls were covered with peeling, mildewed wallpaper. The flooring was cracking, rotted by woodworms. It was caked with dust, formed over years of not being cleaned.

Doug brushed the dust off his coat. The only light source came from the moonlight shining through a single large oval window in the center of one wall. The moonlight oozed through the glass, providing just a bit of light.

As he studied his surroundings in the dim light, he suddenly made out the shadow of a body. It was small, that of a young child. "Ivy," he screamed. The body did not move. He began to move closer to the body. Every step he took, the colder his blood went.

As he drew closer, he could see the body more clearly. It was a small boy. He stopped in his tracks. A creaking floorboard sounded behind him. His breath slowed down and he slowly turned to the sound.

There was nothing there. He turned back to the boy. "Hello," he called. Still no movement. Doug moved closer. A sudden wave of nausea hit him at the smell of rotten flesh.

The House

Against his better judgment, Doug moved closer to the body, the stench becoming more overpowering with every step. Doug reached the boy. As he knelt down, a sense of revulsion overcame him, knowing what he was about to face.

Doug placed both hands on the boy's side. With a swift motion, he pulled him over to expose his front. Doug, unable to control himself, hurled at the sight.

The poor boy was clearly dead. His eyes were white; the light had been drained from them. There were deep ligature marks on his neck. His face had begun to decompose; maggots slithered across the flesh. The whole lower jaw had been eaten away, with the jawbone exposed. Doug had never seen such a sight.

Doug fell backward onto the floor. He closed his eyes tightly, trying to erase the image from his mind. However, he was not alone with the boy. A sudden chilling laugh echoed from the other end of the room. Doug looked up, his heart pounding in his chest.

From the shadows of the room, a gruesome woman appeared. Her eyes were empty, just lifeless sockets. However, her mouth was not stitched together.

"Who are you?" Doug stammered from across the room. Her mouth twisted into an evil smile.

"Don't tell me, Douglas, that you don't know me by now," the woman whispered with a ghastly smile.

"Nanny Moon," Doug replied.

"Good, Doug, good; you learn fast."

"Where is my daughter?"

"And what makes you think I have your daughter?" she said, the smile still on her face. "Why would I want to abduct a young, beautiful child like Ivy?" she asked, with a chilling emphasis on *beautiful,* drawing it out too long.

Doug's body filled with rage. He moved closer to Nanny Moon. "I know you are involved," Doug accused her.

Nanny Moon began to cackle; every cackle chilled Doug's bones. "You think you have it all figured out, don't you?" She smirked. "You've been listening too much to that stupid Miss Black."

Doug shook his head in disagreement. "You're lying," Doug shouted.

"Ok, you got me," she said with a surprised tone. "I did steal your little rat." Her facial expression shifted to anger. "You didn't make it very challenging for me. Black did warn you to leave before it was too late." Moon moved closer to Doug. She appeared to glide across the floor. "Ivy even told you she was being threatened, and you still ignored her poor little soul."

"What have you done with Ivy?" Doug screamed again.

She stopped a few feet in front of Doug. Her smile was still ablaze, her eyes glinting with pure evil. "She is in a safe place," Moon whispered. "For now. But I can't promise to protect her forever."

"Why are you doing this? She is an innocent child," Doug asked, a tear rolling down his cheek.

"Look at you you're pathetic! A pathetic little man," she hissed in return. "No one is innocent in this world, and you ask why, why!" she screamed. "I was murdered oh so brutally, so now it is my mission to haunt that house as long as it stands on this earth."

The House

"You were killed because you killed two children. You deserved what you got. It's a shame your soul did not burn in hell," Doug sputtered.

"Like I said, you think you have it all figured out." She went silent, the evil smile still on her face.

"Where is she?" Doug screamed, moving even closer to Nanny Moon. He was close enough to smell her, mixed with the stench of rotten flesh and a feeling of despair that hung heavy in the air. She did not reply to Doug's question. "Answer me," he shouted again. She continued to smile at Doug with no speech.

"Daddy!" A young girl's voice came from behind the ragged, eyeless woman. Doug's eyes darted toward the back of the room. Ivy stood behind Nanny Moon. Her pajamas were covered in dirt, and they were ripped to shreds. Her face and hair were also dirty, and small cuts and bruises covered her face, arms, and legs.

"Princess!" Doug screamed, running toward her. A sudden searing pain rushed to his head. He felt a hard fist striking him and throwing him into the air. He landed hard on the ground. He felt his teeth smash together as his jaw scraped along the wooden floor.

"No, please!" he screamed as he turned to look at Ivy. She was gone, vanished.

"You didn't really think I was going to let you take her, did you?" Nanny Moon snickered. Doug looked up her eyeless, dead face, only inches from his.

"This will be your last friendly warning. I would leave while you still can," she hissed.

"I'm not leaving until I get my daughter back," Doug yelled in Nanny Moon's face.

Doug tried to get up, but felt a sharp thud that pushed him back to the floor. She moved her face slowly toward his, tilting it to one side like a bird, her grin coming back. "Your daughter is mine. See you around, Doug." Throwing her head back, she let out an evil cackle.

Doug awoke screaming and throwing his arms around. "Doug, Doug," Joanne said. Doug focused his sight on his wife. She stood above him, her hands on his arms, trying to restrain their thrashing movements.

"Doug, what is the matter?" Joanne screamed at him.

Doug shook his head, trying to clear the lifelike nightmare. "I'm fine. Just a nightmare," Doug replied, turning over. Joanne returned to bed and lay at his side. She soon fell back to sleep, most likely from the calming effects of the pills she taken earlier. Doug couldn't sleep. He shivered as he looked out the window into the darkness, the images of the nightmare fresh in his mind.

21

Two days passed after Doug's nightmare. No new leads had arisen. The police search teams had found nothing in the woods or surrounding area. They had sent divers into the lake to dredge the murky waters. However, they found nothing.

Doug had been assisting Detective Philips with local inquires. He greatly appreciated that Philips was letting him help out. It gave Doug a sense of purpose, a sense that he was doing something to help.

Joanne had been very distant over the past week. She had been keeping to herself, spending most of her time in the bedroom, only coming out for lunch or tea. When she did come out she seemed ghostlike, expressionless, and not speaking much.

Doug knew this was how she was dealing with the ordeal. Doug had been keeping his mind on one thing and one thing only: finding his daughter. Whereas Joanne had withdrawn, his method of handling the agony was to be involved.

Raine had been quiet also, spending most of her time in her room playing with her teddies and watching *Frozen* on the television. She had asked once or twice when Doug came in to check on her.

"Have they found Ivy yet, Daddy?"

Every time she asked this question, he felt a little piece of his heart breaking. "Not yet, Princess, but they will, I promise." After this reply she would look disappointed and continue playing with her toys.

The interviews of the very few neighbors in the area had so far turned up nothing, nothing at all.

"Well, that was the last neighbor on the list," Philips said as he heaved himself into the car.

"And not a single one knows anything about Ivy's disappearance," Doug moaned, slamming his fists on the dashboard.

Philips glared at Doug. "Calm down, Doug. No need to start slamming things."

Doug shook off his sudden feeling of rage. "I'm sorry. It's just so frustrating. Someone must know something," Doug said, looking at his feet.

"Well, it's coming to the end of day. Probably best I get back to write up the reports about nothing," Philips said, disheartened.

Doug nodded. The sense of needing to get home had overcome him. He wanted to see Raine and check on his wife.

"How is Joanne doing?" Philips asked as the two whisked along the country lanes to Doug's house.

Doug sighed. "She's doing ok, I guess. She has been moping around the house, not speaking much."

The House

"Have you tried talking to her?" Philips said, looking in Doug's direction.

"I've tried speaking to her, but she hasn't really said much in return," Doug replied.

"Hmm…I'm sure she will speak to you when she is good and ready," Philips said with a reassuring smile.

Doug returned the smile, and then turned to watch the mountain and forestry scenery passing by in a blur.

They soon came to a stop outside Doug's home. "Thanks again for your help today, Doug," Philips said, patting him on the shoulder.

"No problem. I'm happy to help gets me out of the house," Doug replied as he opened the car door.

"I'll be in touch," Philips said.

Philips backed up the driveway in reverse, soon disappearing from view. Doug walked into the house, his body beginning to sweat and his brain beginning to sear with pain. The urge for his pleasure rose to his conscious mind. His blood was pumping and raging through his veins. His body temperature was rising, his skin hot.

Doug burst into the house, losing his footing. He stumbled into the wall, knocking down a photo. He hurried to the kitchen and began throwing open the cupboards, searching for his pleasure. His conscious voice was quiet, but Doug's ugly passenger was very vocal within.

You've had a tough couple of days, Doug. Just sit back and relax. Doug, listening intently to these commands, closed in on the bottle of vodka. The beautifully sculpted bottle sat perfectly still, singing his name like a siren luring him in for the kill.

Doug moved closer, the taste of satisfaction already in his mouth. Doug grabbed the bottle and ripped the top off. He retired to the armchair in the study and sat, pouring himself a small glass. The essence slid down his throat, slithering straight into his bloodstream. His passenger screamed with satisfaction, loving the feeling. Doug poured himself another drink and tossed it back.

Doug remembered the first time he had again lifted a bottle of vodka to his lips. It was a couple of days after the incident had taken place. People in the area were talking about him. A local postman had been spreading the gossip on his rounds.

"Have you heard about Douglas Moore from number forty-eight?" he would say to the occupants of every house on the street. "Terrible business. That poor family. People are saying it wasn't an accident. I swear to you on my mother's grave, God rest her soul, it wouldn't surprise me either. I always thought he looked a bit dodgy."

These types of rumors were everywhere in Doug's old town before he moved his family away. Each day he would walk to a nearby shop to pick up a morning newspaper and a toffee crisp bar. People would stare at him from their houses, giving him dirty looks and then drawing their shades. It was really unnerving.

Joanne was suffering too. Coworkers at her previous job had closed ranks on her. They ignored her, made her feel unwanted. After one particularly hard day at work, a few days

The House

after Doug had been let go from his job, Joanne had returned home, her eyes flooded with tears.

"I've had it up to here, Doug. I can't take it anymore. We need to move."

"Move…move where?" Doug said, not knowing what to say.

"Anywhere, anywhere away from this place. It's full of backstabbing, two-faced bastards!"

"Joanne, calm down. We'll get through this."

"How? How are we going to get through this, Doug?"

Doug felt the anger building inside him, and he walked out of the room to stop the situation from escalating any further. He headed for the backyard. As he approached the back door in the kitchen, he saw the bottle of vodka on the alcohol rack. He remembered pulling it out of the rack and taking it out into the evening summer air. It was the first time he had tried vodka. The burning sensation as it slid down his throat felt good. It helped him in a way that he did not understand. He remembered taking another gulp and then another and another, until he was steaming drunk and passed out, sprawled in the rear lawn in the flowerbed.

He was awoken the next morning by sweet little Ivy. She poked him hard in the ribs, which brought him into the present world. His head pulsated with pain.

"Daddy, are you ok?" she asked, her beautiful blue eyes staring at him, with a hint of concern.

"Oh…hello, baby. Yes, Daddy is fine. Daddy just fell asleep outside."

"Why?" Ivy asked.

"Because your daddy is a silly, silly man," he said with a cheeky grin. Ivy noticed him joking around and beamed back. Her adorable smile made Doug feel ashamed that he had let himself be found like this. However, even worse was that his body was screaming for more alcohol, yearning for that burning feeling in his throat that had helped him forget about his troubles.

"Daddy, are you sure you're ok?"

"Yes, baby, I'm fine. Now come here and give Daddy a great big bear cuddle."

She laughed. "You'll have to catch me first, Daddy." She broke into a run, making a run for the house. Doug stood and postured himself like a big bear and started growling as he chased Ivy into the house. She screamed happily as he grabbed her around the waist, lifting her into the air.

He pulled her in tightly for a giant bear hug. She giggled playfully and then turned around to face him.

"I love you, Daddy,"

He smiled at her lovingly. "I love you more, sweetheart." Doug kissed her on the cheek and then set her down. "Now go and play with your sister go on."

Doug felt a tear trickle down his cheek as he relived that memory and continued to drink. With every glass he consumed, the more the horrifying images of Ivy, scared and all alone, went away. The world began to spin in a drunken blur. The walls became like tidal waves swelling around him. His vision was beginning to go black. He passed out in the chair.

The House

Doug awoke from his drunken sleep; Joanne was shaking him violently. "Doug, Doug, wake up! Wake up!" she shouted. Doug's vision started to focus. Joanne was holding a candle. The house was pitch black. For some reason, the lights were off.

"What? What's wrong?" Doug said, tormented by the pain in his head. His brain felt like it was being pounded with a hammer.

"The power has just shut off," Joanne said, concerned. With some difficulty, Doug got up out of the chair. He could hear the wind blasting against the house. Rain thundered on the roof like little shells exploding on the tiles.

"It's the storm. It's most likely knocked the fuse box out," Doug said, rubbing the back of his head.

"Babe, can you please get the electricity back on?"

Doug sighed and made his way to the front door. Unfortunately for Doug, the fuse box was situated in the front garden. He pulled on his raincoat and opened the front door. The wind was twice as loud outside. The trees waved unsteadily as the wind pounded against them. The air was humid, however, not like previous nights, with the bitter cold.

Doug, pulling his hood over his head, went out to battle the storm. The rain assaulted Doug, as if it were attempting to tear through his raincoat. He zigzagged across the forecourt toward the fuse box, dodging the small ponds forming in the gravel.

Reaching the fuse box, he pulled the box cover off, peering at the inner dials. He noticed that they were all connected correctly. He was puzzled. The power must have gone down in the whole area; that was the only explanation. He began to head back to the house. The wind blew against him as a feeling of someone watching him engulfed him. Looking around, he saw nothing but the trees blowing in the roaring wind.

He shook his head and continued to the house. All of a sudden, the storm lifted, the wind dying off completely and the rain retreating into the heavens above. Doug looked around. It was silent-not a single sound. Suddenly, in the distance, he heard the chilling sound of a piece of rope swinging. Joanne appeared at his side.

"The storm has stopped," she said, joining Doug. Doug held his finger to his mouth, bringing her to silence. The swinging sound continued. Joanne listened intently, tilting her head to the side like a cat. "That sounds like a swing, a rope swing perhaps," she said.

"I don't think it is," Doug said. He began to walk toward the side of the house. Joanne followed him. Doug looked out at the army of trees in front of him nothing.

Doug and Joanne looked at each other in confusion. "Strange," Joanne said, shrugging her shoulders. She turned, walking back to the front of the house. Doug remained for a moment, looking at the tree line.

A sudden soul-frightening scream came from the front of the house. It was Joanne. Doug, his blood turning cold, ran to his wife's distressing screams. As Doug came around the corner, he saw his wife kneeling on the ground, her hands over her mouth, screaming frantically.

The House

Doug crouched down, holding his wife and looking into her eyes, which were filled with pure horror and distress. "Honey, what's wrong?" Doug shouted over her screams. She did not reply. Her eyes were firmly fixed on something behind Doug. "Joanne, what's wrong?" Doug asked again. No answer. Her gaze was transfixed.

Doug, confused, turned to look at what Joanne was focused on. A chilling tingle threw itself up his spine. His mouth dropped at the sight that was before him. The hairs on the back of his neck screamed to attention, tingling in fear.

In front of him was something hanging from the large oak tree. It was a body, a small body. It was a body of a young girl, a girl Doug knew well. It was Ivy, her body limp and lifeless.

Doug let out a cry of horror, scrambling to the oak tree. Her body was too high for him to reach. He looked around for a ladder or something to help get her down. Nothing. Doug noticed something wrapped around her neck. It was a sign with a horrifying message: "You had your warning." Doug's legs went weak. He fell to the ground, tears streaming from his eyes, the tears leaving wet tracks down his cheeks. Joanne was still screaming in the background. Doug's heart was bleeding inside. The pain of his daughter's death ripped at his insides.

His world was collapsing around him. Doug's eyes now burned with the tears building up. He then collapsed on his back, screaming into the air. Back at the house, all the lights sprang back into life.

22

Philips awoke from his deep sleep. The telephone was ringing, vibrating violently. The room was blurry. Philips rubbed his eyes, the room now coming into clear view. Philips's room was large, with an oak desk in the far corner holding his home iMac.

Philips got to his feet, wearing nothing but his boxers. His phone was still shrieking to be answered. "Hello," Philips grunted, picking up the receiver.

"Detective Philips," a young female voice returned, "it's the control room." Philips looked at his clock. Three thirty in the morning.

"This better be important," Philips said, sighing.

"Yes, the FIM is requesting you head to the Moore house," she replied.

Philips's attention was immediately captured. "Why, what's happened?"

"I'm sorry to say that Ivy's body has been found outside the address."

Philips felt his body go cold. "I'll be right there." Philips hung up and threw on the nearest clothes he could find.

The House

Ten minutes later, he was hurtling down the country lanes, his unmarked Passat purring along. All he could think about was getting to the scene before any evidence was lost.

He reached the driveway to the house. Local units were already at the scene. A young officer waved him in. He drove down the drive, and the sight that followed turned his stomach. The small body of a young girl could be seen hanging from a rope.

Philips pulled up outside the house. He jumped out of the car in a rage. "Why is this poor girl still up there?"

The local officers looked at one another in confusion. "We were waiting for the force medical examiner," one officer replied.

"The doc will be able to do her examination without the poor girl being strung up still. Cut the poor girl down."

"Medical examiner is here," an officer shouted from the gate as a vehicle approached. It was doctor Faye Lungfield, an infamous force medical examiner. She was disliked by many officers. She exited the vehicle. She was a short woman with dark-black hair and horn-rimmed glasses. She was pale, with pursed lips and a stern look.

"Detective Philips." She nodded in his direction, walking past him toward the body. Officers were in the process of pulling Ivy's body from the tree. "Who told you that you could move the body?" she shrieked at them.

"I did," Philips said coolly.

"And who said you could make that call?" she growled.

Philips looked at her in disbelief. *God you're a bitch,* he thought. "Last time I checked, Doc, I don't answer to you. The family doesn't need to see their child in this manner."

Lungfield spun on her heel, sighing in defeat. Philips left her to it and went to inspect the tree. The noose had been left in situ for CSI to photograph the scene.

The branch was still intact, with no tears in the bark. Doug looked down and started inspecting the earth around the tree stump. No footprints. Then he saw it two rectangular indents in the soil, as if someone had placed a ladder to aid in getting the body up to the branch. "Can you take pictures of this, please?" Philips asked. The CSI operator took some photos of the marks in the soil.

"So, what is your assessment, Doc?" Philips asked. She didn't reply straightaway. She just stared into Ivy's lifeless eyes.

"Doc."

"Sorry, yes, time of death I would estimate to be seventy-two hours ago."

"Seventy-two hours?" Philips said, astonished.

"There are scrape marks on her heels and feet, which would suggest she was dragged to this spot, and she was then hanged."

"I can't believe this. There is no way she could have been here that long without being noticed," Philips said.

"That's your job, Detective," Lungfield hissed. "I'll know more about the cause of death after I've done the postmortem."

"Ok, thanks." Philips moved away from her, walking to the house. As he walked through the door, he felt uneasy.

The House

This was the part of his job he did not like doing: speaking to victims' families.

Doug was in the kitchen, his head buried in his hands. His shoulders quivered as he sobbed. Joanne was nowhere in sight. Philips walked over to Doug. "Doug," he said softly.

Doug looked up at him, sniffing and wiping away his tears. "Gary, sorry. I didn't see you standing there."

"There's nothing to be sorry about," Philips replied. "If you're feeling up to it, I would like to ask you a few questions."

"Yes, of course. Do you need Joanne to be present?" Doug asked, sniffing again.

"Only if she is feeling up to it."

Doug walked back into the study. "Joanne can you join me in the kitchen for a moment, please?"

Without a word, Joanne emerged. Her makeup was all over the place, her mascara dripping down her face. Her eyes were bloodshot from crying.

"Mrs. Moore, I'm so sorry for your loss," Philips said, offering his hand.

She smiled weakly and took his hand. "Thank you," she mumbled.

"If you're feeling up to it, I need to ask a few questions," Philips said, taking a seat at the table by Joanne. She nodded sheepishly. "Thank you. Now, the medical examiner is going to be conducting a postmortem, as there are some anomalies in Ivy's cause of death."

"I think Ivy's cause of death is apparent, don't you think, Detective?" Joanne spat.

"Mrs. Moore, I'm sorry to inform you that Ivy's time of death was diagnosed to be seventy-two hours ago."

Doug looked up in concern. "Seventy-two hours? There is no way she has been hanging there for that time."

"I agree," Philips replied. "From the preliminary examination, it appears that Ivy's body was dragged from somewhere else."

"Do you know where from?" Doug asked, sitting up in his chair.

"Not yet, but I'll get the best search team officers on the job."

Joanne laughed. "Oh, because they did such a bang-up job the first time."

"Joanne, please," Doug said.

She glared at Doug. "Doug, it is their fault our beautiful daughter our beautiful Ivy, is never coming back, will never play with her sister again. They have left us a broken family." With that, Joanne, tears now flowing, stood and stormed out of the room.

"I'm sorry, Gary. She didn't mean that. We both know how much you and the officers have done to find Ivy," Doug said, looking at Philips.

"No, she's right. I let you and your family down. I let Ivy down," Philips replied. "I promised to get her back, and I failed to keep that promise." Philips looked at Doug, his face full of guilt. "But one thing I do promise, whether it kills me or not, I will find the person who killed Ivy, and I will bring the monster to justice, I promise you that."

23

A week had passed since the Moores had found Ivy's body. Doug had spent his days overcome with grief. It came in waves, engulfing his senses, overwhelming him at times. His brain was strangled by the distressing images of the death of his daughter. The family had received many letters offering condolences. There was a rainbow of flowers in the study of different sizes and colors. The days had ached on. Neither Doug nor Joanne had spoken much to each other.

Joanne had spent much of her time in their bedroom sleeping. Doug had tried a few times to get her out of bed. However, he was met with resistance each time. Raine had taken to her room, not speaking to Doug at all. Doug had never really talked to her about death; it was such a hard concept for a child to understand. When he had told her the news about Ivy, she cried endlessly for hours, not letting Doug or Joanne touch her or console her in anyway. Doug had been making the funeral arrangements. He had decided that Ivy would be buried in Saint Mary Magdalene Church in the village nearby.

On the day of the funeral, Doug stood at the bedroom mirror, inspecting his black suit, which was comfortable and easy on the eyes. He also wore a crisp, white shirt and a black tie. He tightened his tie and walked into the bathroom.

Joanne was nowhere to be seen. "Joanne," Doug called. The sound of running water came from the shower. Along with it came the sound of a woman sobbing. Doug moved over to the shower, pulling the curtain aside. Joanne sat on the shower floor, her head in her knees, crying her heart out.

"Sweetheart," Doug said, turning off the shower. "Come on; let's get you out of the shower."

"I can't do it, Doug. I can't go. I can't say good-bye to her. My heart is breaking." Joanne looked up at him, her skin wrinkling from the water.

"Joanne, I know this is tough…but surely you want to say good-bye to Ivy," Doug said, placing his hand on her knee for encouragement. She looked into Doug's eyes. He could tell he was not going to be able to persuade her. "Well, maybe it's a good idea that you stay home with Raine. I think she's too young to come to a funeral."

"Am I a bad person, Doug?" Joanne spluttered, her eyes forlorn.

Doug pulled her out of the shower to her feet. He gave her a tight, loving embrace, kissing her forehead. "Of course not, Joanne. We've both had a tough couple of weeks. Just get some rest."

Doug helped Joanne back to bed, tucking her in. Before leaving, he opened the bedroom windows. The room was

The House

musky and full of despair. He left the room, walking into Raine's room. Raine stood by her wardrobe, getting changed into her dress for the funeral.

Doug felt himself about to cry. "Princess." Doug cleared his throat. She turned and ran to him throwing her little arms around him. Doug lifted her into his arms, cuddling her tightly.

"Daddy, are you ok?" she asked, wiping a tear away from his eyes, her touch warming his cheeks.

"I'm ok, Princess. Now, I need you to stay home with Mummy," Doug said, placing Raine down on the bed.

"But Daddy, I want to come with you."

"I know, darling, but Mummy is not well, and I need you to look after her. Can you do that for me?"

She stared at him for a moment, and then nodded in reply. Doug beamed at her, kissing her on the forehead. "Thank you."

Doug descended the stairs, grabbed his coat, and left the house. The weather had cleared up since the storm had passed. The air was light, with the hint of winter. It was late November, and the last of autumn was dying off, about to be replaced with bitter cold. He stepped into the courtyard, the hairs on his neck standing up in the cold. The morning sky was ocean blue, not a cloud in sight.

Moments later he was driving down the lane toward the church, where he was to meet with the funeral directors. Saint Mary Magdalene Church was located in the rural village of Cerrigydrudion. It stood in the center of the village, looking toward the village square on one side and the breathtaking countryside on the other.

The church itself wasn't very large. Its foundations were made from stone, with a Welsh slate roof fitted above. The graveyard was large and not crowded with gravestones.

Doug pulled up in the lot. A few friends of theirs stood in the lot, talking in hushed tones. Doug noticed that Joanne's parents hadn't come. They hadn't spoken to Joanne for nine years due to a family fallout, the cause of which had never been explained to Doug. Doug's parents were also not present. However, they had a good reason. They had both died in a terrible boating accident in the south of France, when Doug was only fourteen.

Doug got out of the car and began walking to his friends when he noticed a car pulling into the lot. It was Detective Philips. He exited the vehicle and walked over to Doug. "Good morning, Doug. I'm sorry for your loss," he said, shaking Doug's hand.

"Thank you," Doug replied gently. "I didn't know you were coming."

Philips nodded, smiling slightly. "I attend all the funerals for any murder I investigate, out of respect."

"I appreciate that very much." A group of Doug's old work colleagues arrived and came over, offering Doug their prayers and wishes.

"Where is Joanne?" Philips asked, looking around for her.

"She wasn't feeling up to saying her good-byes. Truth be told, I'm not feeling up to it myself," Doug replied, his

The House

sadness clear in his voice. From the gates of the church, a man wearing elegant white robes and a black vestment with golden stitching walked over to them.

"Good morning, Vicar," Doug said, holding out his hand.

The vicar held Doug's one hand in both of his. "Good morning, my child. I'm sorry, but it's time," he said in a calm, soothing voice.

Doug drew in a deep breath and walked into the church. The inside of the church was bright. Sunlight beamed through the stained glass windows, casting a prism of colors into the church. The casket stood at the far end of the church. The vicar stood at the altar, overseeing the congregation. A substantial amount of lilies surrounded the casket.

The service was beautiful, although it was painful for Doug. The guests sung the hymns that Doug had chosen. Then it came time for Doug and some of the undertakers to carry the casket out. Doug stood up from the pew and walked to the casket, his hands beginning to sweat. He linked arms with the pallbearers. Doug felt his heart pounding in his mouth, his legs becoming weak. Doug could feel the tears escaping from his eyes. All his thoughts were on his beautiful child inside. His hands, tightening around the casket, embraced his daughter for the last time.

The group soon stood at the freshly dug grave. The casket was lowered slowly and respectfully into the earth. The vicar stood at the grave, speaking out to God. Doug stood at the edge of the grave. He pulled out a small teddy. *Ivy's favorite.*

His fingers began to tremble, the bottom of his lip buckling under the pressure of his grief.

"Mr. Moore, if you wish to place anything with her, please do so now," the vicar said with an encouraging smile. Doug felt all of the group's eyes on him. He took one last look at the teddy, his mind taking him to the days that Ivy's little hands held this very teddy. He remembered how she would bring it to the dinner table and pretend to feed it, and how she would cry if they forgot to bring it on long trips.

Doug could feel his eyes filling with tears again, the memories of his daughter getting more and more powerful. His thoughts of the good times cast a faint smile amid the grief.

A hand on his shoulder brought him back to earth. "Doug, it's time," Philips said. Doug let out a moan as he threw the teddy into the depths. He felt the feeling of loss course through his body, bringing him to tears. Philips kept his hand on Doug's shoulder for support. Doug was glad that someone was supporting him.

The service ended, and Doug thanked all the guests for coming. He stood and spoke to the vicar for a short time and then thanked him. Philips waited for Doug. "What are you going to do now?" Philips asked as they walked to the lot.

"I'm not sure. Go home and check how Joanne is doing," Doug replied.

"Send her my regards. I'll pop over in the next day or so. Need to go through the report that has come back from the medical examiner," Philips said, waving. He got into his car and drove away.

The House

It was silent now in the lot-not a soul in sight. With this, Doug got in his car and drove home. The whole way home, all he could think about was the sign he found on the body. Come to think of it, the detective had not mentioned the sign at any point since his daughter had been found.

Doug arrived home and was greeted with a shocking sight. He froze on the spot, unable to move or speak. On the wall of the hallway a message had been written. But this was not in ink, no it was written in human blood!

24

I'*M COMING FOR YOU*. The heart-stopping message froze him where he stood. Doug stood there for what seemed like hours before the feeling came back into his hands.

Doug pulled out his mobile phone and dialed.

"Hello, Detective Philips."

"Gary, it's me, Doug. I need you to come to the house," Doug said.

"Why? Is everything ok?" Philips asked, concerned.

"Just come, you need to see this."

"Ok, ok. Take a breath. I'll be there in ten minutes."

Doug stood there for the entire time until Philips arrived, just like he said, ten minutes after the call. He came to Doug's side, looking into the hallway.

"What is it, Doug?" Philips said, not looking in direction of the message. Doug pointed, his arms shaking, to the wall. Philips looked and blinked continuously, as if he couldn't believe he was seeing what he was seeing. "My god, who would do such a sick thing on the day of a funeral?" Philips shook his head in disgust.

"I think I know who has done this," Doug said, staring into space. Philips turned to look at Doug, his eyes

The House

twinkling at the possibility of a lead. "Nanny Moon," Doug said, his eyes darting toward the threatening message on the wall.

Philips looked blankly at Doug for a moment, his face shouting disbelief. "Doug, I know you've had a rough time, but you can't be serious," Philips said with a confused tone.

"Of course I'm serious. Who else would do this?" Doug said coldly.

"Doug, it's clear that some psychopath is stalking your family," Philips said, looking closely at the written message.

"I had a dream the night before Ivy's body was found," Doug admitted. *I'm going to have to tell him,* he thought.

"What kind of dream?" Philips asked.

Philips stood there in disbelief as Doug told him the tale of his dream. He also told Philips about the night he discarded the doll, how he hit the spirit of Nanny Moon on the road, and the threatening message she had written on his car window. Doug looked at Philips's responses. *He thinks I've gone mad. Maybe I have,* he thought.

"I don't believe it. There is no way a ghost has risen from the dead to stalk and kill a small child and then threatened to harm the rest of the family," Philips said in astonishment.

"There is only one way to find out. We need to visit the grave of Nanny Moon," Doug said.

Philips started shaking his head. "No, I don't think that's a good idea."

"I'm going to find out the truth, with or without you," Doug said, walking out of the house.

"Doug, wait. I see that this means a lot to you, and there may be something with this Nanny Moon business," Philips said, looking into Doug's eyes.

"Thank you, Gary, I really appreciate it," Doug said with a small smile.

"So, where to?" Philips said.

Doug thought for a moment, and then it clicked. "Belinda Black. She knows where the grave is. Maybe she'll take us to it."

Philips nodded in agreement. The two men walked from the house into the dark forest. The trees were still covered in ice from the incoming winter. The shack belonging to Black was as dark and creepy-looking as ever. This time Black sat in the creaking rocking chair on the porch, staring in Doug and Philips's direction. An evil grin warped face.

"Well, well, look who's come back," Black said.

"Miss Black, we need to ask you a few more questions," Philips boomed as they walked up to the porch.

"More questions? What am I to you?" she hissed.

"If you want to be, you could be a main suspect in a murder case, unless you answer my questions," Philips warned.

"Main suspect." Black chuckled. "I'm almost eighty-five years old, and you think I could heave a child up a tree and hang her from it?"

"How do you know how she was found?" Philips replied.

"You don't think I could see all the police cars with their lights shining from the lake? I walked past the house to have a look." She giggled. "What questions do you have, Detective?" she said, sounding bored.

The House

"Last time we spoke, you mentioned the death of Nannette Moon." Philips began reading his notes.

"Ahhhh, so now you believe me about Nanny Moon."

"Miss Black, I'm in serious need of some answers," Doug said, distress clear on his face. "My daughter was murdered, and I think that this Nanny Moon may have something to do with it."

Black looked at Doug for a moment and then started cackling. "Oh, please, get me a violin," she said, holding her stomach as she laughed.

"Doug, I'm not having her disrespect you like this. Let's go," Philips said, his anger mounting.

"Oh Detective, get a sense of humor, please," she replied, chuckling. She looked at Doug. "What do you want to know, Douglas?"

"Nanny Moon. Where is she?" Doug demanded.

She laughed again. "Like I've said in the past, you don't find Nanny Moon. She finds you."

"So you're telling me that no one knows where she is?" Doug asked.

"Douglas, she is a spirit, not a living person. Spirits aren't easy to find," she returned. "I do, however, know where they left her body and where the family decided to bury her."

Doug looked up at her, intrigued. "Go on," Doug said.

"I'll have to show you. I need a walk anyway." She got to her feet, pulled on a raggedy old cardigan, and picked up her walking stick. She stumbled down the steps, banging her stick as she went. "Are you coming, or am I walking up there alone?"

Doug and Philips looked at each other for a moment and then decided to follow her.

For an eighty-five-year-old woman, she was fit. She was fast on her feet as she led them through the woods. The closely entwined trees stood before them like an obstacle course. However, they were no match for her. The flat woodland ground began to rise, the pitch getting steeper and steeper. Black was not fazed at all. Doug, on the other hand, became breathless. *God. I'm terribly unfit.* His chest bulged in pain as he heaved.

"Come on, Douglas, don't tell me that an eighty-five-year old woman is in better shape than you." She laughed.

"Can't say I'm used to walking up mountains every day," Doug retorted. The woodland was getting lighter the higher they went. The sunlight started streaming through the canopy of branches above, which was getting thinner and thinner with every step.

They broke through the tree line suddenly, now standing before a meadow at the base of a small mountain. A path led through the open field, and they could see that it climbed to the summit of the mountain. Black started on the path, with Doug and Philips behind her.

They soon reached the top, where the path ended in a small clearing. In the center of the clearing was a strange pile of rocks. They were not arranged neatly or in any particular order-just a bunch of rocks in a jumbled heap.

"Welcome to the grave of Nanny Moon," Black said, resting against the rocks.

The House

"You're telling me she was buried under these rocks?" Philips said with disbelief.

"That's for you to find out. I've said too much already."

"What is that supposed to mean?" Philips said, turning to look at her. Black had disappeared into thin air.

"What the hell? That woman gives me the creeps," Philips said, shivering slightly.

Me too! Doug thought. Doug did not reply to Philips as he inspected the stones. *Her gravestone, perhaps.* There was no sign of any obvious disturbed earth in front of the grave.

"Doug, even if this is Nanny Moon's grave, it's not been disturbed. I think we're running into a dead end," Philips said softly.

"No, it's definitely her! She's stalking my family and me. She killed my daughter!" Doug raged. "I will find something here even it takes me all night."

Philips watched while Doug combed the gravesite, looking for some sort of disturbance in the earth, any sort of clue. Nothing. "I don't understand," Doug shouted, slamming his fists against the rocks.

Philips moved closer to Doug. "Listen, today has been a long day for you," Philips said with sympathy. "Come on, Doug, let's go."

"Ok. Maybe it's for the best. I need to check on Joanne," Doug said with disappointment.

Doug and Philips walked back to the house in silence. The trip down the mountain was much easier on Doug's chest.

Doug walked into his hallway as Philips drove away. The message still gleamed on the wall, the blood shining in the light. Doug's stomach churned a little. A sudden chilling breeze whistled out of the house through the front door. He turned, only to feel the chill come back in through the door, slinking its way up his spinal cord and hitting the tip like an explosion under his skin.

His heart now leaped into his mouth. A shout tried to escape; however, no sound came out. In front of him, the study was tipped upside down. Books were strewn across the room, and the rainbow of flowers had been ripped to shreds and scattered across the floor. The leather chairs had been thrown on their sides.

He heard the sudden sound of footsteps walking on the top floor, and the distant sound of an evil woman cackling could be heard from outside the house. Without warning, an all-too-familiar bone-chilling scream came from upstairs. The scream belonged to Joanne.

25

His wife was screaming again-the same horrified scream as when she found Ivy's body. Doug threw himself up the stairs, his hairs prickling with fear. His heart felt like it was in the grip of an iron fist; he could feel it pumping in his neck.

He burst into Raine's room, where Joanne's screams were coming from. What lay in front of him made him physically ill, and his knees gave way. He fell to the floor. "Oh my god," Doug shouted into the air.

Raine was nowhere to be seen. Her bed was covered in blood. Her dolls and teddies were ripped to bits. The most distressing sight was on the ceiling. Another message was written in blood: *I HAVE HER NOW. TIME IS RUNNING OUT.*

Doug got to his feet and ran to Joanne's side. "Joanne, what happened?" Joanne was shaking uncontrollably. Her face was pale; the blood had drained away. Her hands were covered in blood. "What happened to your hands?" Doug asked, grabbing hold of them.

"I...I...I ran into the room and slipped, and I landed in the blood," Joanne stammered.

Doug looked at Joanne's clothes, which were also covered in blood. "What happened before that?" Doug said, pulling Joanne closer.

"I heard Raine shouting. She was talking to someone. At first I thought it was you, but then…" She started wailing again. "I heard Raine saying, 'No, get off me,' so I ran into her room, and you know the rest."

"Oh my god, this can't be happening not again," Doug said, his mind racing with panic.

Looking around the room, he noticed the bedroom window was open. Doug ran to the window, looking out into the garden. The night sky was closing in, the sun a fire blazing on the horizon. The breeze bellowed into the room. Screams could be heard in the wind. *Raine's screams?* Doug wondered.

He listened more intently to the screams. They sounded like a young girl's. "Help, help, Daddy! Come and save me." The screams were getting louder.

"I'm coming, sweetheart; Daddy's coming to save you," Doug shouted into the wind.

Joanne looked at him in confusion. "Who are you shouting at, Doug?" she asked.

Doug looked at her, not quite understanding. "What do you mean? You can't hear Raine screaming for help out there?"

Joanne listened intently and shook her head. "No, I can't hear anything," she replied.

The screaming was getting louder and louder in Doug's ears. "Raine, I'm coming! Hold on," he shouted again, running out of the room.

The House

"Doug, wait! Don't leave me alone," Joanne shrieked.

"Joanne, I've got to save Raine! Call Detective Philips and get him down here before we run out of time."

And with that, he was gone. He ran out the door into the courtyard. The screaming was coming from the woodlands toward the south shore of the lake. Doug ran to the pebble beach; nothing was in sight. Then he saw a gruesome sight: one of Raine's shoes, soaked in blood. He ran to it, noticing a trail of blood leading over the dam walkway toward the woods. Doug followed in pursuit.

26

Philips sat at his desk, looking through the postmortem report from Faye Lungfield. The report stated that Ivy Moore had been killed seventy-two hours before her body was found. The cause of death was asphyxiation, and the possible method was described as a pillow. Some fibers from a pillow-type material had been found in her hair.

He sighed, throwing the report down on his desk and rubbing his eyes. Suddenly his office phone rang. "Detective Philips," he answered.

"Detective." It was the high-pitched shout of Joanne Moore. "I need you! Raine has been taken! The evil bastard has taken her."

Philips couldn't believe what he was hearing. "How long ago was she taken?" Philips asked, jumping to his feet.

"About ten minutes ago," Joanne replied. "I saw her about thirty minutes ago."

"Right. I'll get local officers and the dog unit," Philips said, grabbing his car keys. "Where is Doug?"

"He thinks he can hear Raine screaming. He's gone after her," Joanne said, panicked.

The House

"Ok, stay calm, Joanne. Officers will be with you soon," Philips replied.

Philips moved to the door of the office. He pulled his radio out. "TA from DELTA 2166, urgent."

"Go ahead."

"I need all local officers to head to the Moores' house. Their second child, Raine Moore, has been abducted. I need a dog unit also to assist in the search."

"Roger, FIM is going to confer with silver command."

Silver command was the next stage of the hierarchy within the police control room. Usually a chief inspector would liaise with the FIM on high-stakes events.

Philips, now in his vehicle, raced to the scene. *How could this happen twice in a couple of weeks? This is crazy,* he thought. But there was no time for thinking; he had to get to scene. He could see blue lights ahead as he pushed his vehicle to its limits.

Philips turned into the Moores' driveway. The dog unit was at the scene, where the handler was sifting through large amounts of leads all twisted together like writhing snakes. Inside the dog cage in the rear of the car, a dog was eager to get out and start tracking. Officers were talking to a frantic Mrs. Moore.

"Detective, why aren't these officers searching the woods? My husband is out there alone looking for Raine," she said.

"Joanne, calm down. Officers," Philips said, looking at three officers in the courtyard, "I need you to follow the dog handler on his search and assist him in any way you can."

The officers and dog handler hurried into the woods.

"Detective," a young officer said as he appeared from the house. "Sir, I think you should come and take a look at this."

Oh no, what now! Philips thought, dreading what he was going to see. He followed the officer. He was taken upstairs into Raine's room. Sergeant Lomax was already at the scene.

"Detective, I've never seen anything like this before," he said, a look of fear on his face.

Philips now knew why. The message on the ceiling was enough to strike fear into anyone. "Mr. Moore has gone after what he thinks is his daughter screaming," Philips said.

"Well, I hope for his sake he doesn't come across whoever did this," Lomax said, now looking toward the crimson-red carpet.

"I know. Me too," Philips said, looking out the window. "Get me the force medical examiner down here. Let's start processing this scene."

27

Doug continued running, his heart pounding. It was pitch black. Raine's screams filled the forest air. The red mist controlling his legs pushed him forward, ensnaring his senses. Tunnel vision blinded his sight. His ears concentrated on one thing and one thing only: the screams of his child.

The screams were getting louder and louder and closer and closer. "I'm coming Raine! I'm coming," Doug screamed, his lungs straining under the weight. He suddenly realized that he recognized his surroundings. The ground began getting steeper and steeper. He knew where he was. The tree line broke. The top of Bron Bannog was silent, the moonlight shining down on the grave of Nanny Moon.

Another scream from Raine came from the side of the grave. "You," Doug yelled in rage. Standing next to the grave was a tall, hooded figure wearing black, tattered robes. The dead face of Nanny Moon was hidden beneath the hood, half illuminated by the moon. Doug felt an icy hand grasping at his heart.

A creepy grin glittered in the moonlight. "Help, help, Daddy. Come and save me," she returned, imitating Raine's voice perfectly. Doug's heart dropped as he realized the trickery. "Aww, poor Dougie-Wougie, did you fall for my little trick?" Her grin was getting wider and wider.

"Wh-where is my daughter?" Doug stumbled over his words.

"She's safe," Moon replied, still smiling. "For now. For the moment, it's just me and you."

"What do you want from me?" Doug screamed.

"I just wanted to see if you are going to leave yet. Or are you going to put Raine's life at risk too?" She smiled.

"You killed my four-year-old girl! You strung her up like she was nothing," Doug cried, moving closer to Moon.

"Waah, waah, poor Doug. I did your little parasite a favor. Took her away from this cruel, cruel world," she said, a hint of sorrow in her voice. "Look what happened to me. I didn't deserve that. This world is unfair."

"She was a child. You didn't even give her a chance to live her life."

"You know nothing about living life, Douglas. You spend most of your time drinking your life away when your wife isn't watching, hiding who you really are. A drunk. A waste of space," Moon hissed. "And you should talk! You think I don't know about the little incident you got yourself into?"

Doug knew what she was referring to. His mind went back to the day of the incident. He moaned in upset. "That was an accident!"

"Yet you hide it from everyone you come into contact with-pretend like nothing happened-and you have the cheek to criticize me."

The House

"I regret everything that happened that day, but don't act like you're punishing me for that day. You're not killing my family to punish me," Doug said. "You're punishing my family for something that happened to you in the nineteenth century."

"Those people blamed me for murders I did not commit. They took my eyes and sewed up my mouth, leaving me for dead on this rock. So, yes, I've cursed that godforsaken house, and until my spirit is finally repaid for its sacrifice, I'll carry on killing you and your little family." Evil shadowed her face now, the sorrow from her tone evaporating into the night sky.

"Where is Raine? I'm warning you," Doug said.

Moon clenched her clammy, wrinkly fingers against her teeth. "Oh, I'm shaking, shaking in my boots," she mocked. She pulled her fingers away, seemingly proud of her mockery. "And what are you going to do about it, Dougie?" she asked in a childlike voice.

In a rage, Doug spat on Moon's gravestone and then kicked it, dislodging one of the stones.

She stood there for a moment, looking in dismay at the stone that had fallen. Her head then slowly creaked in Doug's direction, her face painted with rage. "You disrespect me," she growled.

Doug, noticing her anger, spat on the grave again.

"How dare you!" she shrieked like a banshee. Doug's eardrums collapsed under the pressure. She lunged for Doug, the earth churning up as she steamed toward him. Doug realized his mistake and stood rooted, unable to move.

The pain crashed into his body like a wave, toppling him over. He fell onto his back in the cold, damp grass. Before he knew it Moon was on top of Doug, smothering him. He grabbed hold of her arms. The skin was just flesh, and the stench oozing into his nostrils curdled his stomach.

He felt the sudden, searing pain of jagged teeth piercing his flesh like a knife cutting into meat. Doug could feel the blood escaping from the puncture wounds being burrowed into him. Blood now seeped out onto the ground, soaking the grass. Her claws sank farther and farther into his flesh. He could feel his bones crunching under the sheer power. Doug closed his eyes, the blinding pain causing him to cry out. Knowing he was in trouble, Doug mustered all of his power, lifted his legs to Moon's chest, and kicked her backward.

Doug used the time to get to his feet, scrambling forward. He broke into a run, noticing too late that the ground dropped away just in front of him-a cliff edge. Before he could stop, he felt the weight of Moon crashing into him from behind.

Doug fell to the ground and tumbled off the cliff. As he went over the edge, he noticed a large tree trunk sticking out of the earth. He grabbed it and held on for dear life, stopping his fall. He could feel his legs dangling as he held on. "Help!" he screamed. *It's hopeless. No one knows where I am.* Below him he could hear the rushing current of a snaking river, the rapids booming against the large rocks in the riverbed.

Doug looked up, only to be greeted by the horrifying sight of Nanny Moon's rotten face. She smiled at him as he

The House

helplessly struggled to hang on. "Well, well. Aren't we in a pickle?" she joked.

"Please, please don't," Doug begged.

She smiled again. "Let me tell you something. I killed Ivy, I'm going to kill Raine, I'm going to kill Joanne, and, you guessed it, I'm going to kill you. But Doug, I'm going to save you for last." She smiled. "Your death will be slow and painful." Moon was quiet for a moment, peering into Doug's frightened eyes.

Moon turned her face when she heard the sound of men shouting and the police dog barking in the distance. "Well, I've got some important stuff to do," she said, and then disappeared.

Doug sighed in relief, and began looking for a way to climb back up to the surface. Then Moon's ugly face returned, smiling even more. "I'll see you soon, Dougie." She patted him on the hand. Then she dug her nails into his flesh, the pain making Doug scream and release his grip from the tree trunk. "Safe trip," Moon screamed, mocking him with evil laughter.

Doug was falling, falling through the cold air. The cliff rose to about forty feet. His clothes flapped as the wind slapped his body as he fell. The wind was cold, stabbing his eyes and cheeks. All his life's accomplishments and regrets flashed before his eyes.

The rushing river was getting closer and closer. Doug braced for impact. His body crashed into the water, instantly being carried in the fast rapids, which pulled him under. The water was freezing, taking Doug's breath away. Panic was setting in. He had no energy to look for a way out. *It's so cold.* Doug could feel his blood freezing.

Then he felt a thud as his head smashed into a large rock situated deep in the water. Doug's world went black.

28

Philips stood in Raine's room. CSI was taking pictures of the message on the wall and the blood-soaked carpet. Doctor Lungfield had been at the house for around an hour now. She was assessing the carpet by pulling out bits of fiber and placing them into a small cylinder.

"Doc, have you got anything?" Philips said. He thought, *God I hope you do. I've got nothing.*

She stood up, shaking her head. "I need to take some of these samples I have collected and test them," she said, putting four vials of blood into her briefcase. "One thing I will say, Detective, is that if all this blood belongs to Raine Moore, taking into consideration her age and height, there is no way she is still alive."

The news sent a chill deep into his bones. He didn't want that to be true. Lungfield bid him goodnight and left. Philips noticed Joanne walking up the stairs. Her face was haunted with depression, which appeared to be gripping her very soul. Philips walked to her, noticing that she was barefoot and that her feet were covered in dirt.

"Joanne, where have you been?" Philips asked, stopping her on the landing.

She looked at him angrily. "Where do you think I've been?" she hissed. "I've been out looking for my lost child, the only child I have left."

Philips looked closer at Joanne's legs, which appeared to be covered in old scars and some fresh lacerations. "Mrs. Moore," Philips said slowly. "Have you been self-harming?" he asked, pointing at the scars.

She looked up at him, embarrassed that he had noticed them. "Has anyone found my husband yet?" She changed the subject.

Philips decided not to press her on it. "No, no one has seen him yet."

"God, I hope he is ok." Her anger subsided, replaced with concern.

Philips's phone started ringing in his pocket. "Detective Philips."

"Hello, Detective Philips, this is the control room. We have taken a call from Denbigh Hospital. They have admitted an adult male by the name of Douglas Moore."

Philips felt his blood run cold. "What do you mean? Is he ok? What's happened?"

"Reports are still unclear. He was picked up by an ambulance. He is reported to have a broken arm and is currently unconscious."

"I'll be right there. No one speaks to him before I do," he barked.

The House

As he turned to tell Joanne, he was met with nothing. Joanne was gone. He had no time to go looking for her. Philips rushed out, telling the officers on scene to keep a close eye on Joanne Moore in case the murderer returned and to inform him if she asked for him. He left the house and got into his car, starting his trip to Denbigh Hospital.

29

Doug awoke in a hospital bed. It had cotton sheets and a plain white duvet. He felt shocked and didn't know where he was. "Where am I?" he shouted like a madman.

A petite young nurse with long, curly blond hair flowing down her loose scrubs uniform answered. "Mr. Moore, please calm down. You may wake the other patients," she said, smiling. Doug looked around. He saw people around him lying in hospital beds, mostly elderly people waiting for the sweet release of death.

"Please help me," Doug pleaded. She placed a hand on his shoulder, soothing him instantly. He looked at her more closely, her beautifully toned skin calming him further. "What am I doing here?" he asked, his tone now calm.

"Don't you remember?" she replied, checking the back of his head. "You jumped off a cliff and hit your head on a rock. It's lucky that you were pulled out of the river by a local farmer."

Doug, concerned again now, placed his hand on the back of his head. He felt bandages covering the wound below, which was tender to his touch. Doug looked into his memory,

The House

and a shooting pain hit him in the ribs as he recalled how he had crashed into the water. Suddenly he remembered why he had fallen forty feet into the river below. *I was pushed!*

"I was pushed. I didn't jump; she pushed me," Doug rambled.

"It's ok, Mr. Moore. Please calm down," the nurse said. "The police are on their way, so you can tell them what happened." She smiled again, and it was clear to Doug that she did not believe him.

"Police!" Doug said.

"Yes, Detective Philips, I believe I was told. Yes, Philips. He is on his way now."

Doug tried to recall the night's events. He was going to have to try to explain this to Philips. *But how?* Doug wondered. Doug didn't have much time to think of a way to explain. The ward doors opened, and in strode Philips.

Philips looked around the ward and broke into a fast-paced walk when his eyes met Doug's. "Doug, are you all right?" he asked, taking a seat on the chair next to Doug's bed.

Doug sat up. "I think so." Doug rubbed the back of his head.

"The doctors have informed me that you were very lucky. You escaped with a hairline fracture to the rear of your skull and a broken arm," Philips said. He noticed a jug of water at the bedside and began pouring himself a glass. "I tell you, you are very lucky to be alive."

Doug chuckled. "I know you're telling me! At one point I didn't think I was going to make it."

"Why did you do it, Doug?" Philips said softly, leaning toward him.

"Why did I do what?" Doug said blankly.

"Come on, Doug. Don't shut me out. Not now. No one will blame you after the week you've had. I'd probably try the same thing myself," Philips said in attempt to console him. He patted Doug's arm.

"Gary, I have no idea what the fuck you are talking about," Doug replied, still confused and slightly irritable.

"You jumped off a cliff, Doug! You tried to kill yourself! How do you not remember that?"

"Listen, Gary, I did not jump off that cliff," Doug began. "I was pushed off that cliff."

"Pushed who pushed you?" Philips asked, leaning farther forward in excitement. Doug told Philips what happened on the top of Bron Bannog. Philips sat there stunned, sipping his glass of water in disbelief. At certain points of the tale, he appeared to believe it, nodding his head, but at other times, he appeared skeptical.

"So let me get this straight," Philips said, putting his glass down. "You were pushed off the cliff by Nanny Moon?"

"Yes, she pushed me," Doug said, clapping his hands. An old woman at the far end of the room looked up from her book and asked Doug to keep his voice down. "Sorry," Doug said, raising his hand apologetically.

"I don't know, Doug. Seems a lot to take in."

"Gary, I'm telling you the truth. I did not try to jump off that cliff. I was pushed off," Doug said, starting to get upset. "You have to believe me."

The House

Philips looked down at his notebook for a moment before looking up at him, smiling. "Look, Doug, I'm not saying that I don't believe you. It's just a hard story to sell, that's all," Philips replied, thinking ahead about telling his superiors that Douglas Moore did not try to take his life but was pushed by a spirit of a dead woman from the nineteenth century. *It's crazy. They're never going to believe it.*

Doug pulled his sleeve up and pulled the bandage away from his arm, revealing a large cluster of small, well-cleaned puncture wounds. "Look at this. She did this to me," Doug shouted.

"Doug, calm down."

"No. I will not calm down," Doug continued to shout.

The young nurse, now very annoyed, stormed into the ward. "Mr. Moore, if you don't stop shouting, I'll have to ask the detective to leave." She stormed back out of the ward.

Philips leaned over and inspected the wound. The flesh had been torn in a very strange way. The blood had dried and was now stuck to Doug's skin like glue. "What's that?" Philips said. He inspected the wound closer. Sticking out behind some rolled-up flesh was what looked like a tooth. Philips picked the tooth out of Doug's arm, holding it up to the light. "Wow, that's amazing," Philips said. "I've got to get this to the lab straightaway." He placed it in a little plastic evidence bag he took from his pocket and sealed it tightly.

"What do you think will come back?"

"Well, I'm hoping the identity of whoever is doing this to your family," Philips said.

"Gary, I've told you already," Doug said, the anger rising to the surface again. "It's Nanny Moon. She is the one who did this to me." He pointed at the wound.

"Well, if that's the case, this tooth should be more than a century old. That way we can better prove that it was Nanny Moon who bit you and pushed you off that cliff."

Doug sighed with relief. He finally felt like he was being taken seriously. "Thank you. I know it sounds crazy, but it's very, very real. I can assure you of that," Doug said, shuddering as the smell of Nanny Moon's rotten flesh returned to his senses.

What happened next shocked both Doug and Philips. The ward doors opened yet again, but this time it was not the nurse who walked in. It was two strange men, both wearing flashy black suits with different colored shirts and ties. The first man was tall and had graying black hair, with an air of importance about him. The second walked behind the first, like an assistant; his hair was more youthful and blond. He had very pale skin, as pale as snow.

Philips spun around when he noticed the men walking toward them. He jumped to his feet, brushing himself down. "Sir, I didn't know you were coming. What are you doing here?"

The first man stopped in front of Doug's bed, leering at Philips. "Superintendent Harris is not happy on the progress of this investigation. Mr. Moore?" he said, turning his attention to Doug.

"Yes," Doug replied, confused even more so now.

The House

"My name is Inspector Howell. This is my colleague, Detective Sergeant Cust." The two men flashed their warrant badges at him and then put them away. "I'm afraid you're going to have to come with us to the station. We have a few questions that we would like to ask you." Doug and Philips looked at each other, both bewildered and concerned.

30

Forty-Five Minutes Before

Detective superintendent Rolph Harris sat at his darkstained oak desk. Piles of stacked papers covered the surface. It was 8:15 p.m., and the room was gloomy and silent. The only light in the room came from a small candle on the side of the desk. Its amber blaze glinted on the walls, casting strange, dancing shadows. The wax slowly trickled down the side of the candle like molten lava.

The room was tightly packed, with not much space to move around. Its far wall was home to Harris's prized possession in his study, his bookcase, which was full of law books and crime novels. Harris sat at his desk, perusing a file. It was full of bold and italic typeface, which was straining his tired eyes; he had not slept for over twenty-four hours. The file was a report from his lower echelon about the murder and abduction of the Moore children. He looked over the evidence, searching for clues as to the possible killer.

Harris had some concerns about the case. Not only did he worry he might be looking at two child murders, but he had

The House

not long ago received a call notifying him of the attempted suicide of their father.

"Superintendent Harris," he had answered when he received the call.

A polite, well-spoken female voice greeted him. "Evening, Boss. It's FIM Inspector Samuels. Sorry to disturb you at this later hour."

"Not a problem, Sarah. What can I do for you?" Harris replied. He had tutored Inspector Samuels when they worked on patrol together fifteen years ago.

"Boss, I've been discussing a case with silver command. I'm sure you are aware of the Moore case?"

Harris sat back in his chair, peering out the window at the orange-draped sky as the sun set over the horizon. The sky was turning dark now, and the moon was starting to shine down on the flowerbeds of Harris's front garden. "Yes, I'm aware of the case. A young detective of mine is looking into it."

"Yes, well, there has been a further development. The father Douglas Moore has attempted to take his own life by jumping off the top of Bron Bannog."

Harris, his attention alerted, jumped to his feet and began pacing his office. "Is he still alive?"

"Yes, he is currently in the hospital, but it looks like he is going to pull through."

"Right." Harris said, clicking his fingers for effect. "I am taking control of this case. I need all the files-everything to do with this case. And I want it faxed to me now. This has gone on long enough."

"Yes, sir. I'll get them faxed over to you right away," Samuels replied softly, noticing Harris's displeasure. The call went dead, and he sat back in his chair, peering out the window.

He sat there for some time thinking about the whole case. It then came to him: the father had tried to take his own life not long after the discovery of the second child's abduction. That seemed fishy, very fishy. With this in mind, he began to flip through the file from page to page until landing on the postmortem. Harris was now wide awake. His wide eyes whizzed across the page, reading the detailed report. His eyes landed on the time of death, which showed seventy-two hours before discovery. The girl was smothered with her own pillow. His suspicions became even more heightened.

It hit him so suddenly. He was reading the witness statement that Joanne Moore had provided about the disappearance of her child, Raine Moore. She had told the officer taking the statement that she thought Raine was talking to Mr. Moore at the time of the disappearance just before she heard her screams. All the facts were now thundering around his brain the suicide attempt of Mr. Moore, the use of the pillow at the home, and the fact that Mr. Moore had been heard talking to the victim just before the screams were heard.

Harris pulled the phone receiver violently to his ear.

A gruff voice answered. "Inspector Howell."

"Thomas, it's Rolph. I need you and Cust to bring in Douglas Moore."

The House

"Mr. Moore? Why do you want him brought in, Boss?"

Harris went on to explain his discovery to Howell, who listened intently to his boss's story and his instructions. "I understand. I'll make my way down to the hospital with Cust now," Howell replied.

"I'm not satisfied with Detective Philips's investigation, so I'm appointing you in charge of the investigation. I want results."

"Yes, sir, of course," Howell said with a hint of satisfaction. The conversation ended.

Harris got up, walked to the bay doors that led to the midlevel balcony, and opened them. It was freezing tonight. The cold air gripped hold of his body tightly like a vise, squeezing all the warmth out of him. He gazed out across the view of the small residential area, with brickwork homes and new builds plotted evenly apart. An elderly man walked his elderly dog, both of them breathing heavily on their short walk.

It was quiet. One of the street lamps down below was shaking in the gentle night wind, its light flickering on and off, putting a small patch of street in and out of darkness. *Oh my god!* Harris was startled.

Harris backed off from the railing. He blinked furiously. *It can't be.* The lamppost went out again. He squinted, concentrating hard on the dark patch of street below. The light illuminated the street again; it was empty. *Must have been seeing things.* Harris could have sworn he saw a young girl with a blood-soaked dress staring up at him.

He shook his head violently, trying to get that image out of his mind. The tiredness was starting to cloud his mind again. *Let's get this bastard and end this horrendous case.* He smiled at the thought that they may have got their man and went off to his bedroom to finally, after twenty-four hours, get some rest.

31

Doug had been rushed out of the hospital. Sergeant Cust allowed him only a few minutes to get changed while he watched. He could hear Gary and Inspector Howell arguing.

"Why was I not consulted about this before the decision was made?" Philips spat. "No one has seemed interested in this case until now."

"The decision came from the top, and from what the super has discovered in a short amount of time, your friend Mr. Moore is now the main suspect."

"Suspect? Are you mad? You think Mr. Moore killed one of his children and then abducted the other?"

"Listen, Philips, I'm now in charge of this investigation, and I want your report, passing over all information about this case," Howell demanded. "And I want it by 23:00 tonight. Do I make myself clear?"

Philips, chastised, his pride damaged, now lowered his head in shame.

"Yes, sir," he muttered.

"Mr. Moore, are you ready?" Howell said, walking over to him. Doug nodded, concerned over what was going to happen next. "Right, come with me."

Doug now found himself in the rear of a Passat similar to Philips's. Cust sat next to him, looking him up and down. "Is this necessary, to oust me from my hospital bed and take me to the station?" Doug asked, looking uncomfortably out the window. The scenery outside was a blur of colors.

"Of course it's necessary. It's perfectly normal for persons of interest to be brought in for questioning."

"Persons of interest? You mean I'm a suspect in my daughter's death?" The conversation he had overheard a short time ago was still ringing in his ears.

"We'll discuss it all at the station," Howell said with a sly tone.

They arrived at the station a short five minutes later. It was a large building, square in shape, with what appeared to be six floors. The windows were large and square, gleaming in the moonlight. The inspector pulled up in a small lot at the front of the building. He led Doug up a long inclined walkway with steel railings on either side. The walkway ended, leading to a small patch of balcony overlooking the lot below.

In front of him was what appeared to be a swivel doorway with large windows on either side of it. The group walked through the swivel door into a large, dull, carpeted lobby. "Mr. Moore, please take a seat while we prepare the interview room," Cust said, pointing toward a plastic-framed, fabric-cushioned chair.

Doug sat down, his palms starting to sweat. His inner voice screamed inside. *You're a suspect! They're going to lock you up and throw away the key!*

The House

His mouth became dry, his throat irritated by a harsh scratching forming in the back. *No, this can't start now not here.* He rubbed his forehead with his sleeve. The back of his T-shirt started to get damp, his back dripping with sweat. *Going to lock you up, going to lock you up.* The scratching in Doug's throat now turned into a burning sensation, like a pile of coals on a roaring fire. Doug got to his feet, his legs wavering as if he were on unsteady ground.

"Mr. Moore." Inspector Howell stood to the side of him. "We are ready for you now." Doug, unable to speak, shuffled forward to the room that Howell was pointing toward.

He stepped into the room. It was a small, cube-shaped room, much like a box. The walls were made from a strong foam material, with a thin red stripe running around the perimeter. This was to protect officers. If a prisoner or suspect was to attack or become aggressive while in the room, the officers could hit the line at any point, which would send a panic alarm to the control room.

Doug sat down at the small, plain table. Cust and Howell sat opposite him. Sergeant Cust pulled out three cassette tapes, all stickered with a different color. One was red, another white, and the last green. He then placed all three into a tattered old cassette recorder. "Ready?" Sergeant Cust asked.

Doug, now roasting hot and feeling the sweat building on his forehead nodded nervously.

"Ok." He shut the tape holders and pressed the record button. "This interview is being conducted in Denbighshire Police Station. The time is 22:30 hours," Howell said, speaking into the recorder. "I am Detective Inspector Thomas Howell. My colleague who is sitting in on the interview is Sergeant Harry Cust. Please state your name for the tape." Howell looked at Doug.

"Douglas Moore," Doug murmured.

"Good. The reason you are here is to be questioned in connection with the murder of your late daughter, Ivy Moore, and the recent abduction of your other daughter, Raine Moore," Howell said, reading from a notebook with prewritten questions. "Now, before I ask you any questions, I must tell you that you are entitled by your rights to have legal representation present. Would you like to exercise that right?"

Doug sat there quiet for a moment, thinking. *Locked up. Throw away the key!* He shuddered. "No, I do not want any representation," Doug replied.

"Ok, let's get started. Where were you at the time of Ivy's abduction?" Howell said, his pen at the ready.

"I was with my wife at a restaurant in Denbigh. Con Amici," Doug said.

"Yes, we looked into that with the manager of Con Amici. He said that you left the building for twenty minutes while your wife stayed inside."

"No, I went outside to the rear garden to have another drink," Doug sputtered, knowing that this might sound suspicious.

"And why would you need to go outside and drink, leaving your wife inside?" Howell said in a sarcastic tone.

The House

"Joanne had gone to the toilet, so I sneaked out for another drink and lost track of time."

"Why would you need to hide outside to drink?"

"It's not easy for me to say," Doug said, his sweat pouring out of his pores.

"Mr. Moore, may I remind you that you are a suspect in a murder investigation."

"I'm an alcoholic!" Doug shouted. "You happy? I'm a sad alcoholic who has to hide outside so my wife doesn't see me drinking."

"Interesting," Howell said, writing in his pad. "When you realized that Raine had been abducted, why did you not wait for the police? Why did you run into the forest alone?"

"Really?" Doug said with disbelief. "You are really asking me that question?"

"Just answer the question, Mr. Moore."

"When I learned that Raine had been abducted, I heard her screams coming from the woods, so I went out there, not wanting to waste any time. I wanted to save my child don't you understand?"

"So without thinking about your safety, you just ran into the woods alone?"

Doug nodded.

"So why did you jump off the cliff, Mr. Moore? Why did you try to kill yourself?" Howell asked.

Doug, now getting agitated, slammed his fist down hard on the table and jumped from his seat. "How many times do I have to tell you? I did not jump off that cliff! I was pushed!"

"Mr. Moore, calm yourself down," Sergeant Cust boomed, getting to his feet. Doug sat down. "Listen, Mr. Moore, why don't you tell us what happened? Why did you kill your child: poor, young Ivy?"

Doug couldn't believe the arrogance of this man. *Who the fuck does this guy think he is?* he thought. "Did you seriously ask me why I killed my daughter, Inspector?" Doug could feel the tears rushing within, racing to the surface.

"Come on, Doug, we both know you did it. You crept into your daughter's bedroom while your children slept, and you suffocated your daughter under her pillow, didn't you, Doug?" Howell pressed on with a determined look on his face.

"No! How could you say such a thing?"

"And then after you killed her, you hid the body. But what I don't understand is why you hung the body days after she was already dead."

"How dare you," Doug said, baring his teeth like a dog delirious with rabies.

"I really don't understand what kind of a father would kill his child in such an evil way. Please help me understand it, Doug."

"How can I help you understand something that I haven't done?" Doug said, looking at his hands, the skin bright red with anger. The blood had rushed to his fingers now, which were clenched hard into a fist.

"Well," Howell scoffed, "if it wasn't you, who was it?"

Doug thought for a moment. *There is no way they are going to believe me,* he thought. Doug decided to play dumb.

The House

"If I knew that, Raine wouldn't be missing, would she?" Doug replied, still closing his fist tightly. He could feel his flesh buckling under the strength of his fingernails.

"Let's not play dumb, Mr. Moore. Where is Raine? What have you done with her?"

"How did you get the rank of inspector? You ask the most stupid questions. If I knew where Raine was, you guys wouldn't be here interviewing me, now would you?" Doug screamed, jumping to his feet, his pupils dilated and his hands shaking.

Inspector Howell stared at him, shocked for a moment. It didn't take long for his sly manner to return. "What I don't understand is why a so-called father like you would kidnap and kill both of your daughters," Inspector Howell said with a snort.

"Like I've already told you, I have done nothing wrong."

"Well it's not the first time you've killed someone, is it Doug?" Howell said, tipping back in his seat. Doug felt his heart sink; Howell was talking about "the incident."

"That was an accident," Doug said, his voice weak.

"He was a child, wasn't he? Only five years old." Doug looked at the inspector, his eyes welling up with tears.

"Listen, I never meant to hit that child. He ran out in front of my car. There was nothing I could do. It was an accident, a horrible accident, and you have no right to bring it up."

A tear fell from Doug's eyes as he remembered that awful day. It was sunny. He was driving down a terraced street with houses on either side when suddenly, a few feet in front of him, a sun-like orange ball bounced into the road. Before he knew what was happening, a young boy followed the ball into the road.

Doug remembered the boy's face, young and innocent looking, with bright green eyes alive with fear, unable to move as he saw the car coming toward him. Doug slammed hard on the brakes, trying to stop the car. He screamed, knowing it would not stop in time. Then came the soul-destroying *thud* as the car slammed into the little boy.

"Those poor parents having to see their five-year-old son like that. I've seen the photos from the scene-they're enough to make a sane man crazy."

Doug remembered the mother kneeling at the side of her dead son, crying her grieving heart out as the paramedics attempted CPR. It was no use. The boy was already gone. The father had been restrained by police officers as he had tried to attack Doug, calling him a child killer. This is what had caused Doug to want to move from the area. *Child killer,* the locals began calling him.

"Like you already know, it was an accident. The police investigators proved that I was not going over the speed limit. And that there were skid marks at the scene, showing I had attempted to stop. There is no way that incident would make me want to kill my own children."

"It destroyed your life, didn't it? It broke you, turned you into an alcoholic crushed with guilt. Maybe carrying around that guilt for so long has sent you mad. And one day you snapped and killed Ivy, and now you've abducted Raine."

The House

"Like I said, I have not done anything. You're wasting time interviewing me while the killer is still at large," Doug said, throwing his arms in the air in frustration. Inspector Howell did not reply to this and slowly wrote on his pad. Doug felt sweat building under his arms, dripping down his side.

"Inspector, am I being charged with anything?" Doug demanded, his face turning tomato red. Inspector Howell looked at him, his sly eyes glinting in the lights of the room. "Sadly, at the moment, we have no evidence that you have done anything, but, mark my words, we are going to find something very soon," Howell spat.

"In that case, if you have anymore questions, you can forward them to my lawyer," Doug said, standing up and spinning on his heel. He threw the door open and stomped out of the interview room. The hinges cracked under the strain.

Philips was waiting for him in the lobby. "Figured you need a lift home," Philips said with a friendly smile.

Doug smiled back and nodded. "Thanks, Gary," Doug said. The two men got into the car and began the journey back to the house.

Doug felt more at ease now that he was with Philips. The dampness had evaporated away, and his clothes now smelled of musky sweat. Doug explained to Philips about the questions that Inspector Howell had asked him. "Unbelievable," Philips replied. His face screwed up in disgust. "I can't believe they are treating you as a suspect."

They pulled into the drive, and the house came into view. "Listen, Doug, get some rest. I'll continue with some investigations. You need to keep your head down, especially now that Howell is involved. He won't rest until you're arrested for the crime he thinks you committed."

Even though he wanted to help, he knew Philips was right. "Ok, be careful," Doug said. Doug climbed out of the car and walked into the house.

32

Philips didn't sleep much that night. He dreamed about finding Raine; however, she was also dead, with an angry Doug standing over the body holding a blood-soaked knife. Doug's anger then changed to happiness, a thin smile stretching across his face. "It was me all along!" Doug shouted, and with that, he lifted the knife to his throat. With one violent motion, he cut open his own throat. Blood sprayed out like a burst pipe.

Philips awoke in his bed; he had kicked the sheets off in his nightmare. The bed mattress was soaked in sweat. It was daylight. Philips looked at his clock 7:45 a.m. He dragged his sweat-soaked body out of bed, heading for the shower. The warm water flowed over his body, and it felt like he had been cleansed of his nightmare.

A bit later, he was sitting at his desk, looking over the report that he had written for Inspector Howell. Philips looked out the window. The weather was overcast but dry.

"Philips, got that report for me?" Howell boomed, walking into the room.

"Yes, sir." Philips lifted the report up, passing it to Howell.

Howell read while standing by Philips. "Hmmm…it will do," he said with a sneer.

The day went on, with nothing eventful or of note taking place. Philips still hadn't received the results about the tooth that they had found in Doug's wound. Around five o'clock in the afternoon, Philips was reading through a copy he had made of the case file for the Moores. He was searching through the file for clues to help back up Doug's story.

He read the report he had written about what Belinda Black had told them. Philips then remembered a detail Black had mentioned about the house that Nannette Moon had been born in. *I wonder if it's still there.* Philips stood up and pulled on his overcoat.

Philips walked out of the station and got into his car. He pulled a map from the glove box. Philips flicked the map to the page that covered Clocaenog forest. Dragging his finger to and fro on the map, he stopped on a small house, or what he thought was a house.

Going over the route in his head, he started on his way to Clocaenog forest. The roads were clear; darkness was settling over the sky. There was not another car in sight. He was soon turning into the woods. The track was bumpy, and eventually Philips had to stop the car, unable to go any farther.

The winter cold clung to his body as he got out of the car. It was dark in the woods. Only a small amount of light escaped through the branches above. The trees echoed his footsteps as he walked along, the faint sound of a strong-paced river roaring in the distance.

The House

As he walked deeper and deeper into the woods, the trees got closer and closer together. He was starting to get the sense that the trees were trapping him. Suddenly the trees stopped dead. He now stood in a dingy, dark, oval-shaped opening. In the middle of the opening stood a three-story house, leaning slightly to one side. To the side was a creaky old willow tree, its bark worn and torn, and riddled with age. Its soul was stripped bare, leaving no leaves upon it.

The house was made from stone, the walls a gloomy gray color. A small brickwork chimney sat above, emitting small clouds of smoke. Ivy drained the life out of the walls, drowning them. The windows were caked in dust, as if they hadn't been cleaned for years. The roof was made of slate and was missing quite a few tiles. An eerie breeze snaked across the forest floor. The breeze crept up Philips's body, making him colder.

Philips moved toward the house, along the way debating whether to call the control room for backup. He decided against it; he didn't want anyone knowing what he was doing. As he neared the door, it creaked open with the sound of ancient wood yawning to life. Philips entered the ground floor, which, like the windows, was covered in dust.

"Hello," he shouted. A small mouse skittered along the floor into his small hole and burrowed into the wall. Silence. A creaking noise echoed from upstairs. He looked up at the landing above, however, and saw nothing. The wallpaper, to Philips's surprise, was still intact and appeared to have not long ago been fitted. Philips then noticed that the flooring didn't seem to be more than a few years old.

A sudden *bang* came from what appeared to be the kitchen. Philips, not thinking about his safety, ran into the kitchen. There was no one in the kitchen. *What is this? Are you playing fucking mind tricks, house?* The walls creaked in response to his thought. Philips now crept out of the kitchen. He walked up the stairs, searching the top floor, which was comprised of two bedrooms and a small bathroom.

He walked into the second bedroom. There was a four-poster bed, which to Philips appeared to have been freshly made. *Someone is living here.* Philips felt his hairs suddenly leap up as if trying to escape his skin. He had the feeling that he was being watched.

He heard the sudden eerie sound of cast iron scraping along the wooden floor. Sensing another presence with him, Philips spun around and was charged at by a middle-aged woman with strawberry-blond hair wearing a dingy, tattered dress and cardigan. The scariest sight was the fact that she was holding a cast-iron axe.

"What are you doing in my house?" she screamed, raising the axe above her head. Philips backed away in fear from the crazy axe-wielding woman. As he moved backward, his back hit hard into the wall, knocking the wind out of him. Having no other choice, he shouted, "I'm a police officer!"

The woman stopped, lowering the axe but still holding it in a defensive stance. "Police? Where is your identification?" she said with an untrusting look. Philips reached into his breast pocket. "Slowly," she barked, raising the axe up farther. "I'm not afraid to use it."

The House

Philips pulled out his warrant card and flashed it toward the woman. She moved closer to him, peering at his ID. Her face changed. Realizing that he was an officer, she dropped the axe to her side. "Detective, I'm so sorry. I didn't realize who you were. I thought you might be a burglar."

Philips straightened himself and smiled at her. "Have you had bad experiences with burglars, Miss…" Philips probed.

"Miss Moon. No, not for a long time after the last burglar who broke in here," she said with a grin on her face. "And he had his hands chopped off. Never saw him again after that."

"I hope you know that it's an offense to chop off people's hands."

"Of course, and quite right too, but I did it in self-defense." She started walking down the stairs. Philips walked after her. She led him into the kitchen. "Can I interest you in a cup of tea or coffee, perhaps?"

"No thank you, Miss Moon. What is your first name, may I ask?"

"Tabitha, Tabitha Moon," she replied, pouring water into a kettle.

Philips was stunned. *Tabitha.* That name repeated in his head. "Interesting name."

"I was given it by my mother, Sandra Moon," Tabitha replied. "Now, Detective, don't tell me you snuck into my house to ask me my name?"

Philips chuckled. "I'm afraid not. I'm here to ask you some questions, if I may questions about a family member of yours."

"Go on," Tabitha replied, a hint of interest on her face.

"Her name is Nannette Moon."

Tabitha stood silent, the blood draining from her face. "Why do you want to know about my great-great-aunty Moon?" she said in a firm tone.

"Her name has come up in a murder and abduction case in a house near Llyn Alwen."

Her face went even whiter, like a sheet of snow. "Nanny Moon is dead. How could her name come up in any such investigation?"

"I'm not at liberty to disclose that information."

"I think you should leave, Detective. I think you should leave now." Tabitha's words came out in a rush.

"Miss Moon, I need any information you have about your great-great aunt. A small child's life is at stake, and I'm not leaving until I get some answers."

Tabitha stopped and looked around as if to see if anyone was listening. "What do you mean, a small child?" she said softly.

"One four-year-old child has been murdered, and another eight-year-old is missing, and Nanny Moon has come up in inquires."

Tabitha, still white, sat at the dusty table and started sipping her tea. "Well, I assume by now you've heard the tale of Nanny Moon from that stupid bat Belinda Black," she began. "Thing is, none of what she has told you is the truth." Philips looked on as Tabitha continued. "My Aunty Moon never harmed those children all those years ago. She was framed!

The House

Once that knife was found in her room, she was immediately taken into custody without them even looking into it, and then she was murdered. They murdered her so brutally."

"What proof do you have that Nanny Moon was not the killer?" Philips asked.

Tabitha moved over to a small dressing table located to the left of her. She opened the drawer, dust falling from the wood as she pulled. She dug her hands inside, pulling out a medium-size book. She slammed the book on the table. The table shook as if disturbed by a small earthquake.

"What is this?" Philips asked.

"This is the journal of Nanny Moon," Philips sat down at the table next to Tabitha. "She was investigating the Hughes family, as she noticed that there were bruises on the children. She came to the conclusion that Mr. Hughes was the culprit, and later found out it was he who had killed the children. She confronted him about it, so he silenced her by framing her."

Philips read the notes that Tabitha was pointing at. *She was innocent,* he thought.

"It is the Hughes family who cursed that house. I don't blame my aunty for haunting it after what they did to her, but the fact that she has killed numerous families over the years I don't agree with."

"Numerous families? What do you mean by that?"

"Well, everyone thinks that all those previous families moved out without a word. Well, they didn't. They were murdered, all by Aunty Moon."

Philips, not liking how this conversation was going, stood to his feet. "Miss Moon, I thank you for your time. You've been most helpful." He rushed out of the house and started the walk back to the car. His phone began to ring in his pocket. Doctor Lungfield. He sighed, not wanting to answer. "Evening, Doc," Philips said.

"Detective, I have some interesting information about the blood found at the scene." She explained the information.

It was as if a freight train had crashed into him. He nearly dropped the phone in shock. "You're certain?" Philips asked.

"A hundred percent. I'm sure," she replied.

"Thanks, Doc." He let the line go dead. *I've got it!* he thought. He ran to the car, dialing Doug's mobile. It rang for a minute before going to voicemail. "Doug, it's me, Gary," he said quickly. "I need to meet you. Somewhere secret. Meet me at the top of Bron Bannog. It's important, so when you get this message, start making your way up here."

Philips rushed to his car, not noticing the dark figure watching him from the shadows. The shadow was holding a walking stick. He got into his car and drove to the meeting place, thinking about the new information the whole way. *How could I have been so blind? It's solved. I have cracked it.*

33

Doug awoke from his deep sleep; he was drenched in cold sweat. He had woken from a nightmare, a disturbing nightmare of an empty village with lots of people hanging from trees. He was then on the floor facing upward. A shadow was standing above him. Before Doug could make out who it was, he woke up.

Doug sat up in his bed, wiping his sweaty forehead. *When will these nightmares end?* he wondered. He got out of bed and walked to the bathroom. His vision blurred as he turned on the bathroom light. As he filled the sink basin, he splashed some cold water on his face. He drew himself up and looked at himself in the mirror. He recoiled in fear and stumbled into the shower door. Doug looked back at his reflection. *Nothing. I'm seeing things.* He thought that he had seen a mangled face licking his cheeks. That wasn't the scary part. The scary part was that he saw his own face.

The head was decaying, with rotten flesh hanging off it, and his tongue was greenish and forked like a snake's. He shook his head violently, getting the image out of his mind. He walked back into the bedroom. Joanne was gone to the world, her bosom rising up and down slowly as she slept.

A small light was blinking on his mobile. He walked over and picked it up. He had a voicemail. Swiping the phone open, he listened with interest to the message. "Doug, it's me, Gary. I need to meet you. Somewhere secret. Meet me at the top of Bron Bannog. It's important, so when you get this message, start making your way there." The voicemail ended. *How odd.* Doug called Philips, noticing his message had been left two hours ago. He received an out-of-service message after a short ring. Doug, curious more than anything, changed into some clothes and left the house.

The weather was poor, slight rain cascading down from the inky-black sky. The wind was slight with a cold bite to it. Doug began his ascent to the top of Bron Bannog. The forest was dark, really dark. The trees in front of him were just shadows. The hair on his neck began to prickle. Stabbing pains like knives cut into his back.

An owl hooted, which echoed eerily through the woods. The branches and fallen leaves whispered in the winter wind. Something did not feel right. His mind was screaming, *It's a trap.* But his legs seemed to be disconnected from his brain, and he continued to walk toward the top of Bron Bannog.

He heard a sudden snap of a twig to his left. His legs now listened to his brain, and he stopped, his feet glued to their spot. Something was in the undergrowth, coming toward him. "Who's there?" he shouted into the air, his voice resounding through the forest. Whatever it was started moving faster, getting closer and closer to him. Doug looked around for something to defend himself with. *Nothing*! His

The House

heart, now poisoned with fear, was beating fast like a tired racehorse. Doug braced himself for what was coming. A ginger fox jumped out of the bush, a dead rabbit for its lunch in its mouth.

Stupid, bloody animal, he thought to himself as he watched Mr. Fox scurrying off with his meal back into the woods. Doug continued the climb and finally came out of the forest, looking out at the grave of Nanny Moon. A sudden, shooting pain rose through his entire body. He screamed in agony, falling to his knees. *Stay away! Don't go one step farther!* his conscience screamed at him.

Suddenly he saw it a strange silhouette near the pile of stones. From where he was, he could not make out what it was. A bone-chilling gust of wind traveled up his back. He shuddered. Doug stood there, his legs shaking with fear, his head beginning to burn in pain.

Doug picked up a nearby stick and raised it in a defensive pose. "Who are you?" Doug yelled. The figure did not reply. "Nanny Moon," Doug yelled again. Still nothing. Doug raised the stick, ready, and jumped to the side of the figure, now realizing what it was. Pure horror invaded his senses. He screamed and screamed like a madman. Falling to his knees, he screamed even more, unable to control himself. His mind was breaking down at the mere sight.

Impaled on a log in the earth in front of the gravestone was a human head that had been severed from the shoulders. The flesh was cut with jagged strokes as if done with a rusty, dull knife. The head was no strangers; it was Detective

Philips's. His blood still dripped onto the grass as if the gruesome act had just been completed. A small crimson pond formed below.

Philips's face was scrunched up in sheer agony. His eyes had been cut from their sockets, leaving whirlpools of blood in their place. Doug hurled up his stomach's contents, still unable to control his shouts of terror. Doug noticed a body lying in the grass a short distance from Detective Philips's head. Next to it was a blood-soaked, rusty knife. Philips's crisp, white shirt was now painted red.

"Fuck me!" he wailed. "I'm so sorry, Gary, so sorry," Doug cried in grief, placing his hand on Philips's rigid shoulders. Suddenly he followed the direction of a whistling breeze, which led him to a message written on the forehead of Philips's severed head: *Should never have left Joanne home alone.* He felt a sudden vibration in his pocket. Pulling out his mobile, he was chilled by the picture that had been sent to him. It was a picture of Doug's house with a caption: *Come and get me!*

Doug, not thinking of anything else but his wife and her safety, lifted himself from the ground. He ran back down the mountain. The wind picked up speed, lashing out at him. It was roaring like a male lion over his kingdom. The trees struck out at him, whipping his cheeks and breaking his skin. None of this fazed Doug, who was committed to getting back to the house.

The house came into view. It was dark and spooky looking. Doug had never noticed its creepiness before. But he now looked hard at it; it was very spooky looking. He ran to the

The House

porch and looked through the window. Nothing. Just darkness. Doug slowly opened the door. It creaked as he let go. Ignoring this, he moved slowly into the house. In front of him, a dim light source was coming from the kitchen. The door behind him slammed shut.

Doug continued into the kitchen. The kitchen light was not on. However, evenly spaced in a large circle on the floor were small round candles, their flames waving like entranced cobras. The circle was illuminating a large cross.

"What the fuck," Doug murmured. The cross was ten feet tall. Doug's eyes trailed up to where the cross nearly touched the ceiling and were confronted with a horrifying sight. Tied to the cross was none other than his daughter Raine. "Oh my god, Raine!" Doug moved to the cross, trying to pull the binding ropes from Raine's wrists. "Damn it," Doug yelled when the ropes wouldn't budge.

"I wondered how long it would be before you showed up," came a voice from behind him. A figure stood in the kitchen doorway.

"You," Doug staggered, shocked. "It was you."

34

In the doorway stood Belinda Black. Her face was slightly fearful. "Why did you do it, *why?*" Doug screamed. Black did not reply. Before Doug knew what was happening, the tip of a knife broke through Black's ribcage, and he heard the sound of her bones crunching against the blade.

Black moaned in pain as the knife was thrust farther into her back. A trickle of blood slipped from her mouth. She looked at Doug, her eyes fading as death was closing in. Suddenly the knife was pulled out and slowly raised to her throat. Belinda gave one swift cry of pain as the knife cut through her neck, spraying blood over the walls. The body of the now-dead Belinda Black fell to the floor, a pool of blood leaking out onto the kitchen tiles.

Now taking her place in the doorway stood another figure. It was hooded, and Doug could not make out the face beneath. "Who are you?" Doug shouted.

The figure began to laugh, which then turned into a creepy giggle. "Sweetheart, don't tell me you don't recognize me."

From the shadows the figure stepped forward, pulling down the hood. The face he was greeted with destroyed him instantly.

The House

"Joanne," Doug croaked, not able to believe it, floods of tears starting to stream down his face. His throat was now dry and painful. "I don't understand. Why…why would you do this?"

Joanne smirked evilly. "You don't think I did this alone, do you?"

Doug let out a shout of terror. Joanne's face collapsed into a rotten, decaying face, that of Nanny Moon, her eyes shrinking into nothing.

"Hello, Douglas," she whispered, smiling.

"I don't understand."

"Well, Doug, I have been working with your beloved wife to play you this whole time. Not that she had a choice." She smirked.

"You mean Joanne?" Doug stammered.

"Yes, Doug, please do keep up. Joanne was the one who abducted Ivy and Raine. It was Joanne who smothered Ivy in her bed, killing her, and she was the one who heaved her body and hung it up on the oak tree."

"No, no, she wouldn't do such an evil thing," Doug screamed, more tears streaming down his face.

"Oh, Doug, she did. And deep, deep down, even though I was in control, she enjoyed every last moment of it." Moon sneered at him.

"Liar! You've poisoned her mind. She loved her children."

"She was also was the one who attacked you at the top of Bron Bannog, I used her body to help me push you off the cliff, nearly killing you." She smiled even more. "I enjoyed killing dear, noble Detective Philips. I'll tell you how it went, shall I?" Her grin widened further as she began to tell her tale.

35

"Evening, Doc," Philips said.

"Detective, I have some interesting information about the blood found at the scene." Lungfield said.

"Go on," Philips replied shortly.

"The blood is not human blood. It belongs to a sheep or a cow. I can't be certain which. But that's not the strangest part. Mrs. Moore told you that she had seen Raine Moore thirty minutes before she was abducted, but problem is that the blood had been on that floor for an hour, at the very least."

"You're certain?" Philips asked.

"A hundred percent. I'm sure," she replied.

Philips was replaying that conversation in his head over and over as he drove to the foot of Bron Bannog. It was Mrs. Moore this whole time. The worst part about this revelation was that he did not understand the motive behind it. His bones quivered at the thought of a mother abducting her own children and killing one of them.

He reached the bottom of the track. He walked up the hill, the trees waving at him in the slight wintery wind. Philips's mind was still racing, unable to get the images out of

The House

his mind. After reaching the top of Bron Bannog, he waited patiently waiting for Doug to arrive. Twenty minutes passed. Philips pulled out his mobile phone, dialing Doug's number, when he heard movement ahead.

Philips looked up and saw a person approaching. It was an old woman holding a walking stick. "Miss Black," Philips said. "What are you doing here?"

"Detective, I need to tell you something. I've seen something that may help your investigation."

Philips was now interested. "What, what have you seen?"

"It's Mrs. Moore. I have seen her." Black started to say; however, she was then struck over the head with a log. Her eyes went dead like stone as she fell to the ground, unconscious.

Standing there was Joanne Moore, still holding the log. "Hello, Detective." Her voice was slightly deeper than usual.

"Joanne, what are you doing?" Philips asked, his blood going cold.

"I can't have you telling on me to Doug. My house presentation is not ready," she hissed.

"Mrs. Moore, I'm now arresting you for the murder of Ivy Moore and the abduction of Raine Moore."

"But it wasn't me," she said, her voice becoming normal again. "Detective, please, I didn't do it!" Her voice changed again, back to the deep female voice. "Silence! How dare you speak? I'm doing the talking." She looked in Philips's direction again, smirking. "I'd like to see you arrest me, Detective."

Philips walked over to Joanne, pulling out the handcuffs. "Such a mistake."

Before Philips knew what was happening, he was thrown in the air, landing on his front. His arms were yanked behind his back. He felt the cold metal of the cuffs clasping tightly to his wrists. "Joanne, what are you doing?" Lying in the grass, he felt a hard fist clamp down on his head, lifting it up to face Joanne's grinning face.

"I'm sorry, but Joanne isn't home at the moment." She grinned even further and began cackling. Her face went straight again. "Now, what should I do with you? I could leave you here helpless, and no one would know you were here. That would give me enough time to sort out my affairs."

Philips tried fumbling in his pocket. He could feel his personal radio in his back pocket. He strained his fingers, touching the tip of the radio. *If I can just reach my panic button…*

"And what do you think you're doing?" Joanne screamed. She ripped his hand out of his pocket. She then pulled out the radio. "Tut, tut, Detective Philips, why would you do something as stupid as that?" she said. She put the radio on a nearby pile of stones and used one of the rocks to smash it into pieces. Philips's heart sank into his stomach. His last chance of finding a way out of the situation was gone.

"Well, you clearly can't be trusted to be stay here." She pulled out a rusty knife.

It sent stabbing pains of fear into Philips's heart. A cast-iron fist blocked his airway, leaving him unable to scream. "Help," he croaked.

She bent down, her face up close to his. She began to giggle. "Detective, no one is coming to save you. Now, sshhh.

The House

Please don't speak. It will be more painful if you do. Doug will be here soon. We will have to get you ready. It's a shame you didn't believe him about me."

Philips screamed in horror as Joanne's face transformed into a dead face, a face with no eyes and rotten flesh.

"Good-bye, Detective." Nanny Moon stood up and pulled Detective Philips's head back.

Philips braced himself. He felt the searing pain of a rusty knife cutting into his neck. He felt his blood seeping out of him. Philips let out cries of tremendous pain. The knife dug farther into his neck. His world was going black as he felt his flesh tearing off the bone. Philips's view went totally black. Death had now taken him from the world, leaving his lifeless, headless body behind.

36

"How could you kill him so brutally?" Doug said, his hand over his mouth in horror.

"I'm not going to lie, Douglas. I enjoyed doing it," Moon spat.

"Why why not me? Why, Nanny Moon, why did you kill my child?" Doug said, tears falling from his eyes.

"Mr. Hughes killed his children, and I paid for his crimes. I chose your wife because I knew it would hurt you, Doug, would crush your soul just before the very end. Your wife also enjoyed killing. She's just as twisted as me."

"No, I don't believe you! Joanne is nothing like you. She is decent and good and pure things that you know nothing about. Joanne, please, if you can hear me in there, baby, talk to me. Tell me this isn't true!"

Moon's face became twisted as if she was holding something back. "Nooo!" she screamed, her head going back in pain. Joanne's face replaced Moon's, her eyes watering with tears. "Doug, please, please, help me!"

Doug moved to her. She placed her hand on his face.

"Please, tell me you didn't do this." Doug wept.

The House

"She has taken over my body, Doug. I can't get rid of her. She killed Ivy. You have to believe me," Joanne said, tears rolling down her cheeks. She had specks of Black's blood on her face, which glinted in the candlelight.

"What are we going to do?" Doug said.

Joanne screamed in pain. "I can't hold her off forever, Doug. There is only one thing you can do." Even more tears flowed down her cheeks. "You'll have to kill me while she is in my body. It's the only way."

"No! There must be another way," Doug cried out.

She smiled back and put her hand on his face again. "Baby, there is no other way. I don't want her to harm Raine."

Doug shook his head. "I can't do it."

Joanne screamed out in pain. Nanny Moon's face now replaced Joanne's. "Should have listened to her, Doug." Moon punched Doug in the face, sending him flying through the air. He crashed backward into the kitchen shelf. Feeling slightly dazed, he scrambled to his feet, narrowly missing being hit by a bowl that Moon had thrown in his direction. Doug scrambled over the kitchen island, bolting out of the kitchen. "Oh, you can run, but you can't hide, Douglas," Moon laughed in hot pursuit. Doug ran up the stairs. A hard grip got hold of Doug's ankle, tripping him. His face hit hard against the stairs. "I'm going to kill you, Doug, and I'm going to enjoy it." She started laughing again. Doug, feeling pure anger toward her, kicked out hard, striking her square in the face.

Doug got to his feet and continued to run up the stairs. Moon screamed in anger, her shrieks shaking the house's foundation. The windows in the house shattered under the pressure.

"I was going to kill you quickly, but now I'm going to kill you oh so slowly," she roared as she climbed up the stairs, her feet pounding on the floorboards. "I'm going to cut off your limbs one by fucking one." Doug ran into the bedroom, looking for an escape route. He could hear Moon reaching the top of the stairs.

Doug climbed out onto the balcony, shutting the door behind him. He started to climb across the ledge on the side of the house, trying to reach the side window. Doug reached out and grabbed the handle of the window. Then a clawlike hand smashed through the glass, yanking on Doug's arm and pulling him toward the now-shattered opening.

"Not how I wanted to kill you, but it will do," Moon sneered, a look of disappointment on her face.

Doug resisted her grip. Doug punched Moon in the face again and again. Finally, with all the power he could muster, he smashed Moon's head against the wall. She let go of him, howling. Doug grabbed her around the shoulders and pulled her out of the window.

She screamed as she fell from the window. Her arms waved as she went. There was a loud *thud,* and Nanny Moon landed hard on the concrete below. Doug ran back down the stairs, jumping the last few steps. His heart pounded in his chest, tears building. He had just thrown his wife out of a window. Raine now came back into his mind. He ran back into the kitchen.

The House

"Raine," he shouted. He tapped his daughter's shoulder and began to shake it vigorously.

Raine's eyes began to flicker, opening slowly. "Daddy," she whispered. "Daddy, is that you?"

"I'm here, baby. I'll get you out of here." Doug searched the kitchen for something sharp to cut the ropes to free Raine.

"Looking for something?" a voice hissed from the side of him. Doug spun around and saw Nanny Moon standing in the kitchen doorway. She was holding a kitchen knife. She grinned. "You really thought that throwing me out of a window was going to kill me?"

Her grin now turned sour. She lunged at him, the knife raised for attack. He found the closest thing, which was a vodka bottle. He picked it up and threw it at her. It exploded on impact, the vodka flying out in all directions, shocking her body.

The slight distraction gave him the time to run for it. He ran for the doorway again. However, he was struck hard in the throat, sending him to the floor. He choked, his throat burning with pain. Doug tried to stand but was punched again, throwing him against the kitchen window. The window smashed. A sharp shard punctured his shoulder. Doug screamed in pain as the shard stuck out of his shoulder blade.

"That looks like it hurts, Dougie. Want me to help you out with that?" she said, laughing. Unable to move due to sheer agony, he couldn't defend himself. Moon wrenched the glass out of his shoulder. Doug cried in pain again. Moon dropped the shard on the floor and raised the knife to his face.

"Now, how about we cut out your eyes and then your tongue?" she said.

"Daddy," Raine screamed, now fully conscious.

"Shut up, you little rat," Moon screamed, facing her. Doug, with his one free hand, picked up a piece of sharp glass, thrusting it into the back of Moon's head. She yelled, pulling out the glass. Doug was now free from her grasp.

"You little bastard," Moon screamed. Doug lunged toward Moon, pushing her to the floor. Doug jumped on top of her, grabbing the knife and wrestling it from her grip, using all the courage and strength he had left.

"Sweetheart, close your eyes," Doug called toward Raine, who wriggled to get free. Moon screamed as Doug used his weight to pin her arms down.

"Joanne, baby, I love you. I'm so sorry," Doug said, the tears starting again. His heart thumped in his chest his hand shook with pure grief.

"I'm going to kill you," Moon screamed. Doug plunged the knife into Joanne's heart.

Moon's face pulled upward. She was screaming in pain. Her face began to shake violently as she wailed. Joanne's face returned; she was in so much pain. Doug dropped the knife.

"Doug, I'm so sorry."

Doug placed his hand on the wound, trying to stop the bleeding. "Joanne, I'm the one who is sorry. Please don't die. Please don't leave me. I can't look after myself without you," Doug cried.

She smiled sweetly at him. "You never could look after yourself." She turned to see Raine still struggling against her

The House

bonds. "Free her, will you, Doug? I want to be able to say good-bye to my Raine," Joanne murmured. Doug picked up the knife from the floor and freed Raine from the ropes.

"Mummy," she screamed as she ran to her mother's side.

Joanne looked at her, placing her motherly, warm palms on her cheeks and wiping away the tears. "Darling, you must look after your daddy and keep him safe."

"I will, Mummy, I promise," Raine replied, a single teardrop forming.

"Doug, promise me you'll look after Raine," she pleaded.

"Of course." Doug held Joanne's hand. "I love you so much. Please don't leave us."

"I love you more, Doug, more than you'll ever know." They embraced, and Doug kissed her lovingly, the last time he was going to get to kiss his wife. As their lips locked, he felt his wife's lips going rigid. Joanne Moore, his beautiful Joanne, was dead. Her eyes now appeared to be at peace.

Doug was crying his heart out as he cradled his dead wife's body, holding on to her tightly, unable to let go. Raine moved closer to his side; she was also crying. Doug looked up and at Raine, who was sobbing even more now. He carefully laid Joanne's body down, closing her eyes. He stood up and lifted Raine up into his arms.

"Come on, Raine, I need to get to the police station." He ran into the courtyard, still holding his child. After putting Raine in the car, he hopped in and cranked the engine. Doug drove away from the house, wiping the never-ending tears away from his face. *It's over; it's all over.*

37

Doug raced along the lanes, still sobbing over Joanne's death. Raine sat in the passenger seat, devoid of emotion. Doug looked out the window at the lake by the house. The water was shining in the light of the upcoming fireball as it rose from behind the mountains. Its heated rays blasted Doug in the face, burning his retinas.

"Daddy," Raine called.

"Yes, baby girl," he replied, looking out the window still.

"It's a shame, isn't it? A real shame." Her voice was getting deeper, more grown up. Doug's heart leaped into his throat, blocking his airway. His hands began to shake. Doug slowly turned to face Raine. Doug screamed. Raine's face was split in half. One side was Raine's face, and the second was the rotten flesh and eyeless socket of Nanny Moon. "Shame you killed the wrong person." She giggled evilly.

Before Doug could move, he felt a sharp knife plowing into his neck. He screamed in pain, feeling the knife tearing into his flesh. He was drowning in his own blood as it gurgled up to the surface.

"Told you I'd get you, Douglas." She plunged the knife farther into his neck. Doug felt his last moments on earth

The House

fading in sheer agony. Death was beginning to engulf him. Blood poured down his front. Doug felt his grip releasing the steering wheel. The car veered off the road, landing on its roof. The car's windows smashed, glass shards flying everywhere. Doug was suspended upside down, the light fading away. Death now took over his body, and his world went black.

38

The police and paramedics turned up at the scene of a nasty car crash. A Volvo was on its roof. Medic Thompson clambered out of the ambulance and ran to the wreckage. The car was a mess. The engine was dead and smoking away. She knelt down, peering into the car through the passenger window.

Inside was an adult male, who was clearly dead. There was a large shard of glass embedded in his neck. His eyes were white with death. Next to him was a sobbing child, a young girl, unable to get out of her seat.

"Hello, sweetheart," Thompson said sweetly. "I'm going to get you out of here. Are you hurt anywhere?"

The little girl shook her head.

Thompson reached into the car, unhooking the seat belt. "Hold on tight," Thompson said with a smile. She helped the girl down and pulled her out from the wreckage. "What's your name, lovely?" she asked, checking her over for injuries. The little girl did not reply. She just looked into space in a trance. She had a few scratches and some bruising on her cheek. "Come on, sweetie. Let's get you to the hospital to get

The House

you checked over." Thompson picked up the child, who had remained quiet, not saying a single word.

She continued with her to the ambulance. The girl looked at the wreckage as they walked away, with her arms wrapped round Thompson's neck tightly. The girl's face peered over her shoulder. "My name is Raine, Raine Moore," she said with one last creepy grin.

Made in the USA
Charleston, SC
25 March 2016